Sojourn

Geonn Cannon

Supposed Crimes LLC • Matthews, North Carolina

Published in the United States.

ISBN: 978-1-938108-98-3

www.supposedcrimes.com

This book is typeset in Goudy Old Style, licensed by Ascender Corporation.

Sojourn

CHAPTER ONE

I. ICE AGE

The stones used for the path were the same white-tan as her boots. The path was wide enough for the four of them to walk shoulder to shoulder without touching, but the three lieutenants accompanying her from the shuttle clustered behind her in deference to her rank. Stretching out to either side of the path were miles of turquoise-blue water. The water had risen to cover the path enough that her boots splashed with each step. The air was crisp with the promise of snowfall and that, of course, was why they had come.

Commander Rani Clare Cossin turned and saw ice cliffs on the far horizon. She had never seen Leucothea in its prime, but she knew those cliffs were relatively new. According to the information packet, the planet was just about to enter its spring thaw. She tucked the collar of her heavy uniform jacket around her neck and focused on their goal. The sensors picked up one life sign, in one of the dozens of huts that stretched out from the city shoreline.

They reached the wide oval area that housed the hut and Clare signaled for the lieutenants to hang back. The structure was made of clay, situated like a hunched spider on the end of the long leg of stone. All but one of the access ports were shuttered against the wind, and Clare took off her goggles. Her canvas cap was pulled low over her eyes and she nudged it up with her knuckle as she stood in the doorway and waited for her eyes to adjust to the darkness.

The sole occupant of the hut was kneeling in the middle of the space with her back to the entrance. Despite the cold, she wore only a thin gown with a gauzy hood that was draped over the pale white curls that cascaded to the middle of her back. Clare knocked on the side of the doorway and said, "Thetis:scholar?"

"That is I."

She turned and Clare saw the woman's profile. In the darkness, her skin looked to be the same shade as the water that surrounded her berth, but Clare knew it was a darker blue. All Leucothean people had blue skin, prompting the derogatory moniker of Blue-Cloths. Her yellow eyes studied Clare before turning back to the brazier in front of her.

"You are from the vessel," Thetis said.

"That's right. I'm Commander Rani Clare Cossin of the PSV *Paralus*. We were hired by your regent to take you to safety."

Thetis made no indication she had heard.

"We'd like to leave as soon as possible, ma'am."

"You may leave whenever you desire."

Clare moved into the room and circled until she could see Thetis' face. "We were hired to take you out of here. We're not leaving you behind."

Thetis pressed her lips together with minor irritation, then looked at Clare. "My regent is reactionary. I am willing to stay here only as long as it remains safe. I am not a martyr. I have seen the same reports as my regent, and I am confident I can remain here for another five months. The summer season is nearly upon us. The temperature will rise before it drops further."

Clare's boots echoed hollowly as she crossed the room to push open the window shutters. Thetis hunched her shoulder and squinted as the light poured in, and Clare pointed at the wall of ice that loomed on the horizon. "See those glaciers?"

"Increased temperatures will hold them back. This planet is my home, Commander."

"I respect that. But you have to face the reality of this situation. Even if summer does hold off the ice, there's a chance winter will start before you're ready. If the city becomes iced, no ship will risk its people or a shuttle to land, and sure as hell no one will risk crossing that path I just walked if it's coated in ice. Summer may have increased the temperature just enough to give you a last chance to escape before you die here, alone. Are your prayers so important that your god wants you to die mumbling them?"

Thetis lowered her head. "Very well." She stood and gathered her robes around her legs. At full height, she was just barely taller than Clare. "We can go."

"You can take a moment to gather your things."

"No. They belong in this holy place. Here, they are sacred. Elsewhere they will just be items. I am ready, Commander."

Clare walked to the pile of clothes in the far corner and rifled through them until she found something heavier than the robes Thetis wore. "Here. Put this on. The wind is pretty bracing, and I don't want you catching a cold."

"I can cope with~"

"*Kest*," Clare cursed. "Are you going to fight about every minor thing?"

Thetis tensed, but took the coat and draped it over her shoulders. She turned and walked out of the hut, and Clare noticed too late that the scholar was still barefoot. She sighed and followed rather than beginning another fight concerning proper footwear. The lieutenants straightened as Thetis exited, and Clare gave them a signal to head back. They had come along at the regent's request, in case Thetis refused to come and had to be taken from her hovel by force. Fortunately it hadn't come to that.

Thetis followed the three lieutenants onto the walkway, and Clare cast one last wary look toward the glaciers. She brought her hand to her lips and spoke into the wrist-mounted microphone of her radio. "Commander Cossin to the *Paralus*. Light the fires; we got her, and we're heading your way."

The response was transmitted in text to the small glass monocle in front of her right eye. She acknowledged and followed Thetis onto the path. They were halfway across when the first fat flakes of snow began to alight on Clare's cheeks and lips. Thetis tilted her head back to look at the sky, then twisted to see if Clare was going to say anything. Clare wasn't petty enough for an 'I told you so,' and Thetis seemed grateful as she faced forward again.

Clare fastened the collar of her jacket and picked up the pace. She wanted to be off the ground by the time the storm started in earnest.

II. Hair's Breadth

The shuttle looked like some subterranean burrowing creature parked between two buildings. The front windows were slightly iced over, and one of the lieutenants had to use a can of wrist spray to thaw the door enough to get it open. Thetis was looking toward the sky, thick white flakes of snow accumulating on her lashes faster than she could blink them away. Clare let her take in the fast-moving storm and then whistled, nodding toward the hatch with her chin. "Come on. We're getting off this rock asap."

Thetis moved inside without comment, and one of the lieutenants pointed her toward a chair she could use. Clare passed Thetis as she was sitting down. "Lieutenant Hass, make sure she's properly strapped in, please." She took her place at the controls and began the preflight. The heat of the engines thawed them enough that takeoff wouldn't be a problem, and she thumbed the communication widget into her ear.

"This is Commander Cossin. We are aboard the shuttle and preparing to come back up to you. Mission was officially a success."

"Glad to hear it, Commander. We'll prepare for departure as soon as you're safely aboard."

Once her team was strapped in, Clare glanced back to make sure Thetis was ready. In her robes and unusual blue skin, she looked completely out of place in the environs of the ship. It was like seeing a tree on a moon. It just didn't fit. But she seemed calm enough.

"Have you ever been in space before?"

Thetis nodded. "Yes. I don't like it much."

Lieutenant Hass smiled as he adjusted the harness straps over his chest. "No one likes it. The best among us tolerate it." He looked at Clare. "Commander Cossin seems to like it pretty good, though. Haven't ever seen her spend more than a day on solid ground."

"You know what they say, Hass. Find somewhere you're appreciated, and lay down stakes. How long until we break cloud cover?"

"Eighty-two seconds."

Clare punched in a new command. "We're taking a little detour. Hang on, fellows." She swung the vessel around so they were facing back the way they had come. The vapor trail from their atmosphere thrusters evaporated against the glass as her lieutenants braced themselves against the hull. Clare turned to make sure Thetis was paying attention. "Take a look, Thetis:scholar."

They were high enough to see most of the inner coast of the continent, the walkways that extended into the ocean looking like matchsticks from so high. The ice covered the majority of the ocean visible from their position, and the land's vegetation was a frosted sea of green. The snow still swirled in the upper atmosphere around them as the shuttle reversed away from the planet. Thetis leaned forward slightly, restrained by the straps over her shoulders and across the waist.

"See that? You still think you could have safely stayed another few months? You think anyone would have risked landing here to pick you up after it got worse than this." She looked forward again and gently swung the ship back to its correct trajectory. "I'm sorry, Thetis, I am. I know this place is your home. The experts say it'll be safe for everyone to return in a decade or so, once they get the orbit knocked back. I know it seems like a long time now, but it'll give you a chance to explore a little. Spread your faith."

"Yes," Thetis said softly. "Thank you, Commander Cossin."

They broke through the clouds and the *Paralus* suddenly loomed before them.

Once they boarded, the shuttle was hooked and ferried into a maintenance berth. Clare escorted Thetis to the habitation area where a room had been set aside for her. She had been silent during the entire docking procedure, and followed Clare through the corridors without a word. At the room, Clare indicated Thetis should hold her hand against the glass panel as she punched in a code that would allow her to use her palm as a key-lock. The door opened and Thetis looked warily into the darkness.

Clare shifted her weight to a more casual stance. "It's really not much different than staying planet-side. We have all the amenities. There's an arboretum if you feel the need for fresh-fresh or sunlight."

"Fresh-fresh?"

"Air. We have artificial circulators, but some people miss the smell of real fresh air."

Thetis nodded. "I believe I will be there often. Do you have... water?"

"There are lakes in the arboretum where swimming is allowed. You have a bathtub in your room, and a shower."

"Thank you."

"I'm just doing a job. The comm is..." She stepped into the room and illuminated a panel on the wall. "Here. If you need anything, just call. A lieutenant or a cadet will be happy to help you."

"And you?"

"Me?"

"If I require your assistance."

Clare smiled. "No offense, ma'am, but I'm the commander of this ship. I led the team to bring you back up here because I didn't want to send some lackey down there to bring you up. You deserved to have an officer escort you. But I don't really interact with the passengers."

"Oh. I understand."

"Have a nice trip, ma'am." She started toward the lifts, eager to be out of her mission clothes and into her ship uniform.

"Commander Cossin?"

She rolled her eyes and then turned.

"You were not simply doing a job. You were employed to retrieve me, but you went beyond that. I have seen what has become of my world, and I have little doubt that your refusal to leave me there has saved my life. Thank you, Commander."

Clare averted her gaze. "It's a job. Enjoy your flight." She turned before Thetis could argue further. When she was alone in the lift, she unfastened the collar of her jacket and rubbed the soft skin of her throat. She looked up at the convex dome of light over her head, squinting into it as she waited to be delivered to the Home level.

She used her palm to unlock the door and stepped inside. An

automated system lit the parlor and dining areas, and the running lights along the hallway to her bedroom slowly came to life with a low amber shine.

A gentle feminine voice came from tiny speakers hidden throughout the space. "Welcome home, Commander Rani Clare Cossin. Would you like something to drink?" She had set her Personal Assistance Matrix to sound like a seductress, so every word came out rife with innuendo and suggestion.

"No thank you, Pam. Music. Picat, Third movement. Ambiance volume."

The piccolo and violin music began to play as she took off her jacket. She took the weapons platforms off her forearms as she walked down the hall to her room, pausing just long enough to hang them in their proper nooks before continuing into her sleeping area. Her mission uniform was bagged and set aside for washing, and took her ship uniform from the wardrobe. Before she dressed, she took the bottle of lotion from her bathroom and applied it to her forearms where the weapons had been secured.

Commanders wore plain white dress shirts with tall collars underneath a leather jerkin. Gold buttons ran down both sides of the leather; men buttoned their jerkins to the left and women to the right. No one exactly could say why, but it was how things were done. Her bone-colored trousers were tucked into knee-high brown boots with a series of buckles down the side, and she tightened them all before addressing her reflection in the circular mirror.

She pinned the gold leaf of her rank on the tall collar of her shirt, brushing her thumb over it to make sure it shined in the light. Women with longer hair had to braid it on duty, but she chose to wear hers short. She fingered the bangs so they feathered across her forehead, and she adjusted her cuffs as she walked back down the hall.

"Pam, music off. Lights off."

The music became quiet, ceasing completely only when she was through the door. The engineers would claim inertial dampeners and the artificial gravity made it impossible, but she could swear that she felt the deck shift under her feet as the ship turned away from Leucothea and began its slow trek to a safe distance before their light-plus engines were engaged. She took a deep breath, oddly more at ease with the processed air than with a true atmosphere, and went back to work.

III. DOWNTIME

The planet's sole inhabitants seem to be arthropod (subphylum chelicerata) with scythe-like appendages which they use to reap their fields. The captain calls them Harvestmen.
~ ship's log, precise date unknown

Gunnery Sergeant Nasim Senech checked his watch as he finished his circuit of the Home level. Two minutes better than his best time. He smiled as he pressed his palm against the glass panel outside his quarters and stepped into his quarters. A burst of air greeted him and he paused to let it cool him off before he continued on to the facilities.

"Welcome back," the Pam unit said in a matriarchal tone. "Congratulations on beating your time, Gunny."

"Always improving, Pam. Is Professor O'Brien on the Wayfarer?"

"Not currently. According to habits, she can be expected to arrive within the next eight to twelve minutes."

"Plenty of time." He undressed in the bathroom and stepped into the shower. He washed away the sweat and then put on a pair of boxer shorts as he returned to the main room. He sat on the edge of the bed and took out the mahogany box he kept in a place of reverence on his nightstand. He took out the small metal diodes and removed the small metal disc that covered the portal on his right temple. He had once used the mirror to make sure he was hooking it up right, but by now he had it down to an art.

Nasim lifted the console from the box and placed it on the bed next to him. The screen lit up from contact with his body heat, and he punched in his password. A few seconds later a line of purple text appeared.

"Been waiting long, hot stuff?"

"I never mind the wait for you," he typed back. "Just got back from a jog. Beat my time by two minutes."

"Well, that deserves a celebration."

"What did you have in mind?"

"Oh, I can think of a few things."

Nasim smiled and pressed a key. His shoulders stiffened, his teeth clacked shut, and his eyes rolled back in his head. The seizure was brief and mild, and he exhaled sharply when it was passed. He lifted one slender black hand and turned it over to look at the palm. Lisa O'Brien was sitting on a couch in her quarters, dressed in a lilac-colored teddy. He curled the fingers and saw she'd painted her nails to match the color. He chuckled in her voice and moved the hands of Lisa's body to the keyboard.

"I like the nails, baby."

Across untold miles of space, in his room aboard the *Paralus*, Lisa used his body to type a reply. "Thank you. You smell good. You're using that oil I bought, aren't you?"

Nasim smiled and typed, "I wear it all the time. Well. Never on duty. I wouldn't survive the ribbing the guys would give me. Do you have the whole night?"

"I have a class in ninety minutes."

"I'll have your body back by then."

"Be gentle with me."

He chuckled, still surprised to hear the familiar sound coming from Lisa's throat in her timbre. "I'll ask you to do the same, Miss O'Brien. Talk to you soon." He activated the away message and stood up, taking a moment to adjust to his new height and body shape. It was a dizzying sensation every time, and he reached up to flip her long straight hair over his shoulders and walked to the bedroom where Lisa kept her toys.

Lisa was stationed on the United Eastern Colony, the head of the science department. Her grandfather had been the pioneer for the Wayfarer technology, so she had been one of the first to volunteer for implantation. It was meant as a means to share information across distances, to share sensitive information without fear of messages being intercepted. Cryptology would be a thing of the past. Nasim's unit was among the volunteers in the first wave, and he met Lisa in the observation house. They hit it off almost immediately and, on her suggestion, began exploring recreational uses for the technology.

Nasim took off Lisa's teddy and turned to look at her body in the mirror. "Mm. Still got it, baby." He brushed his hands over the underside of her breasts, teased the nipples, and then lowered himself onto the mattress to take full advantage of the time he had in her body.

Clare's Capture device was last-but-one generation, a bit clunky compared to the newer models that everyone else preferred, but it suitable for her purposes. Besides, transferring files from one memory card to another could cause image degradation, so she didn't want to risk losing anything.

She slid back to rest against the headboard and activated the device with a sweep of her thumb over the handle on one side. The translucent screen between the handles illuminated, and she propped the pillows against the headboard and reclined against them as the images seemed to appear in thin air just above the screen. She scrolled until she found one she wanted, and she touched it with two fingers to activate the footage.

The small thumbnail expanded and the rest of the menu disappeared. A section of doorway hovered in front of her and, a moment later, a woman stepped through. She was distracted by something in her hands and glanced up, blue eyes widening as she gasped and recoiled one step. She then smiled, shook her head, and tried to block the lens with her slender fingers. Her voice came out of the past. *"Put that away."*

"Not until you do something remarkable."

The hand dropped and the subject now glaring at her now from under a fallen sheath of black-brown hair. *"Oh, I have to be remarkable, huh? You don't ask much, do you?"*

"Come on. I don't have all day. Something remarkable."

They were moving now. Clare was backing up as Laikyn moved across the kitchen, the image wavering slightly as Clare tried to keep it steady. Laikyn returned her attention to whatever was in her hand. For the life of her, Clare couldn't remember what it had been. She was smiling self-consciously and turned so that her hair was obscuring her face. *"You're going to be filming me for a long time, and it's going to be so dull..."*

"You'd waste your whole day just to thwart me?"

"You're worth thwarting. I'm not going to justify this sort of behavior. You're childish."

"I think I'm being conscientious. You're the one being childish."

Laikyn turned and stuck her tongue out. The camera moved closer and Laikyn chuckled as the lens focused on the curve of her neck. The collar of her white robe was hanging open far enough to show the curve of her breast. Above the lens, sounds of kissing were just barely audible on the microphone. Laikyn's hand closed around the lens and put it on the table, showing a three-dimensional image of their kitchen doorway.

Laikyn's whisper was almost lost to the speaker. *"I love you."*

"See? Was that so hard?"

"What?"

"Something remarkable. You loving me? That qualifies."

The camera shifted again, then the image froze. The word REPLAY appeared in the center of the screen, but Clare dismissed it and went back to the menu. She scrolled to another segment of the menu and clicked on the private access screen. She entered her password and picked one of the screens at random.

Laikyn appeared, enough of her upper chest visible to reveal she was topless, and the rhythmic movements of her body left little doubt as to what was happening. She arched her back, black-and-brown hair spread around her head on the pillow like a halo. Her skin shone with sweat, and her face and upper chest were bright red. Her eyes opened just a crack, then wider, and then she turned her head to one side.

"RC, cut it out..."

"Come on." Clare's voice behind the camera was breathless. *"You want to get through those long separations, right? I'll float you a copy. You can watch it in your bunk when we're apart."*

"Rani, turn it off."

Laikyn's voice was serious, so the image cut out in the middle of a thrust. This time Clare pressed the replay option, and she raised the volume. She closed her eyes and listened to the sounds Laikyn had made before noticing the camera was on her. When she started talking, Clare went back to the menu and returned to the public menu.

Laikyn was sitting at a table by the window, writing on paper with an ink stylus. Her sleeves were rolled up to prevent staining them on the wet ink. She looked directly at the camera and stared for a moment, then pointed with her small finger.

"Is that on?"

"Hm? No."

"Clare..."

"I turned it off."

Laikyn stared at it for another moment and then went back to her writing. She casually brought up her left hand, cupped her breast, and then undid a button of her shirt. Without stopping her writing whatsoever, she pulled one side of her shirt away to reveal a pink nipple. She pinched it gently, twisted it until her lips parted in a quiet gasp, then she rearranged her clothes. She looked to her left, where Clare was apparently sitting, and then gave the camera a devilish smile.

Clare paused and returned the smile. She remembered lying in bed the first night she had the camera, toying with the settings and then inadvertently letting it film for the rest of the night. Their first memory card was nearly full of eight hours showing just their bare feet. Clare always meant to over-record it, but she couldn't bring herself to. She watched the footage, zooming through it to watch as they shifted toward, and away, and back together again through the night. When the sun finally brightened their room, Clare's leg had been between Laikyn's.

"There's something on the bed," Laikyn murmured sleepily.

"It's... oh, shit."

Laikyn laughed. *"Has that been filming all night?"*

The image froze and Clare scrolled again. She found footage of Laikyn in a dark tan uniform, the rolled collar of her turtleneck embellished with a shining gold leaf. Her hair was cut short and tucked under a military cap. She cast her eyes sideways, then aimed them forward again to focus on the commencement speech. Her lips remained pressed together, but dimples appeared in her cheeks, the only part of her smile allowed to escape.

Clare closed the Capture and placed it on her chest. She looked at the calendar hanging next to the wardrobe. In thirty-two minutes it would be day 754 since the *Juno's* last transmission, and the last message she'd received from Laikyn. She had it memorized: "Mission progressing well. Nebulas (nebulae?) shining in the distance, so beautiful. Sirens on the shoreline and wax in my ears, love."

Shorter messages hurt more, because Clare knew the only reason Laikyn was being succinct was to keep from crying as she wrote it.

Laikyn was always the codependent one, the one who needed someone to hold her in the night. So as bad as it was for Clare, she knew it was thrice as painful for Laikyn. Out there. Alone.

Clare opened the Capture again and clicked on a thumbnail tagged 'Emergency.' Clare and Laikyn with the long hair both had favored during their Academy days, cheeks together so they would both appear in the image. Laikyn did the talking. *"This one is for you? Okay."* She cleared her throat. *"Yes. I miss you as much as you miss me. More, even. But we're going to hang in there. We're tough. Remember footsteps on the stairs over our heads? Even when we aren't together, we have each other. I love you, Rani."* She turned her head and smacked Clare on the cheek with a big, wet kiss. *"Okay, now you shoot one for me..."*

Clare closed the Capture before the Replay option could appear. She knew if she saw it, she would end up replaying it all night. She hugged the Capture to her chest and closed her eyes, refusing to cry herself to sleep again.

Thetis only remained in her quarters long enough to get a sense of the environs. There was a small portable computer tablet that would provide her with a map of the ship if she got lost, and she stowed that in the billowing pocket of her gown. The automated voice system informed her that passengers could dress in the coverall uniform provided in their quarters or, if they so wished, could continue to wear their own clothing for the duration of their visit. Thetis chose for latter, and lifted her hood before leaving her quarters in search of the arboretum Commander Cossin had mentioned to her.

She had expected it to be as sparse and utilitarian as the rest of the ship, but she was greatly surprised to find a lush garden with meandering canals fed by a waterfall at the far end. She could even hear birds singing in the trees, though she could only catch sight of a few quick flutterings of brightly-colored feathers among the branches. Benches were in abundance, as were tall lecterns with screens that contained information on the nearby vegetation and their planet of origin.

Thetis looked up and saw the vast nothing of space above her. It was speckled with light of faraway stars, and she was swallowed by vertigo for a moment until she focused on the ground beneath her feet once more. She walked the paths until she found a quiet shaded area with lush overgrowth and a wide pool of warm water.

She gathered her robes to her thighs and knelt on the lip of the pond, dipping her hands under the surface of the water. Her eyes closed and her mouth widened in a smile as she submerged herself to the wrist.

She would have put up less of a fight had she known there would be water in space.

CHAPTER TWO

If the Earth was, indeed, a sentient object (as some erstwhile respectable publications would like the general public to believe), surely it was highly offended by our species' eagerness to leave it in our dust. Not that we were the most considerate guests. But the way we fled her surface, like party-goers scrambling to be the first to leave a dull shindig, surely left poor Gaia feeling like the plainest girl at the prom.

In the Fifth Epoch, when technology had advanced to the point to make travel to other solar systems feasible, overpopulation made it necessary. The American agencies combined forces with the Russians and, as a means of forgiving their debt, brought the Chinese in for good measure. These three powerhouses lit off the first rockets and started an irreversible race to get gone as soon as possible.

The United Kingdom funded its own research. While others shot for distance, the UK focused on the general vicinity of the place they had always called home. They annexed the old neighborhood while the rest of us played pioneer.

Left out of the majority of the scrambling, a half-dozen other countries put together their resources and created their own program. They launched as well, joining the AmeriChinRus Agency (ACRA) in shooting for distance.

The juggernaut soon spread its arms wide, like a spider trying to weave a web around the entire known universe and soon forgot about the planet from which they sprung, like children leaving their parent in an old-age home. They elbowed their way into alien politics, continuing their comparison to rude guests at a party (it was their standard behavior, it seemed, no matter where they went in this wide existence). From a small island in a northern sea, a kingdom became the sole proprietors of Earth and its environs. Those who decided to stay behind and eschew the unknown were known as Nests, and they became citizens of the British Rule.

And during these grand strides, a relatively small conglomeration of tiny nations quietly entered the intergalactic equation. Australia, most of Eastern Europe, and a few friendly Middle Eastern countries created an agency called The Peaceful Sea. Their first vessel launched one hundred and sixty-three years after the first transport shuttle was sent out into the cosmos. The Peaceful Sea, despite their name, did not constrain themselves to peacekeeping. The members adopted a militaristic structure and acted as mercenaries, freelance explorers, treasure hunters, provided escort for dignitaries, and occasionally dabbled in less than legal behavior.

Though the Peaceful Sea was the third-place winner in the struggle to reach the stars, they have arguably succeeded far beyond their predecessors.

~ excerpt from Patre' Beckett's memoir *Incomprehensible Ramblings*

IV. DERELICT

Anais Quimby was recumbent in her leather command chair, one boot resting on the edge of her console to keep her balance. As navigator she had the best view on the entire ship; stationed in the Crow's Nest, she could see everything around them with the flick of a switch. A bank of bright screens topped her console, and the top and bottom of her niche were domes of translucent material that let her see the actual space they were passing through. She was human, although her unusual features had caused more than a few misconceptions. Her ears were small and a touch too close to her temples, and her large eyes dominated her other, smaller features and small chin to make her look like a Creff. She didn't mind the comparison. Creff were sometimes given opportunities where humans faced discrimination. The registrar took one look at her large brown eyes and immediately signed the recommendation for her to become a navigator.

Her domain was small, but she made it cozy. Alien flowers hung on daisy chains around the perimeter of the ceiling. Tiny speakers near the floor played music that she controlled from a little platform that plugged into her console. She could go days at a time without seeing or speaking to another member of the crew, and even then it was usually the captain giving course corrections.

She kept waiting to be bored by watching space, but there was always something to look at. Currently the *Paralus* was out in the boonies to pick up some Blue Cloth priestess or something. She watched planets roll by on her screen, then craned her neck to look out the windows to see them with her own eyes. They were beautiful and, seeing them, made her believe in an artisan Creator. He cared for His creations, sure, but in the way that a sculptor loved a statue. Beauty was His goal, and he had more than achieved it. Anais wanted to spend the rest of her life exploring the Masterpiece.

A monitor on her board chirped, and she sank back down into her seat to address it. She re-scanned that area of space and saw what had caused the alarm. "Space junk," she said under her breath, but then she looked again at the shape of the thing. It was big for space junk, and oddly symmetrical. It was something artificial, for sure, but not necessarily worth overlooking. She punched in a change of direction and the ship angled itself toward the object.

"Captain Harp, please."

A few seconds later, the reply transmitted over her headset. "Harp. Go ahead."

"We have an object coming up on up-starboard. I'm changing course so we can get a better look at it. Something seems unusual about the size and shape of it. Estimate a visual in three minutes."

"I'm heading up there. I'll take a look."

She turned and hit the pad next to the door so it would be standing open when he arrived, then swiveled her chair back around to face the console. They had to change their bearing to travel up from their previous position, and then angled to the right until they were facing the right direction. She made the changes gradually so the inertial dampeners could accommodate it. She bit her bottom lip, her hands on the controls and moving as if independent from her thought as she leaned forward to watch for the landmark outside.

Josiah Harp entered the room quietly behind her. His head was shaven, but he wore a bushy mustache that obscured his upper lip and made him look vaguely like a cat. Due to an ocular anomaly, he was forced to wear specially designed eyeglasses so information streamed to his earpiece was projected correctly. Anais liked the captain's spectacles. She thought they made him look classy, like old photos from the Days Before.

He rested a hand on the back of her seat and craned his neck to join her search. When he spoke, his voice was light and joking. "Anything yet?"

"Just about got it, Sir. We're..." Her eyes widened. "Oh, wow."

His tone became serious immediately. "That's one of ours, isn't it?"

The ship was still moving ever so slightly, drifting along on some long-ago decided heading when something had made it stop. It matched their design, so his question was unnecessary. Anais knew he only asked to confirm she was seeing the same thing he was.

She looked down at her console. "We're not receiving any IDEC."

"If there was anyone out there to send it, they would be sending a distress signal as well. Bring us up close. I want to see if we can read the markings before we decide to send a team over. Is Commander Cossin on duty?"

"Aye."

"Good. How far away are we?"

"1.2M kilometers and closing. I should be able to read the side soon."

He nodded. "Contact me when you have the name. I'll have Kira check the registry for any missing or AWOL ships that might have come out this way." He paused at the door. "Good catch, Quimby."

She smiled and increased their speed just a touch. It wasn't every day they stumbled over an honest-to-goodness mystery.

They were four days out from Leucothea, and Clare was finally starting to get her space legs back. Even an hour spent planet-side threw her, and it took a while for her body to adjust back to artificial air and gravity. It was one of the reasons she hated breaking atmosphere so much. Give her a ship big enough to get lost in and she could be happy for the rest of her life. She was in the ship's gymnasium, stripped down to shorts and a sleeveless T. She was dripping sweat, the muscles of her arms straining as she held her feet off the ground for as long as she could bear.

When she reached her peak, she slowly lowered herself until her sneakers were flat on the floor, and she released her grip on the leather handholds which she'd been using to support herself. She was toweling off when Nasim Senech wandered past. The Marine stepped past her and put his hand into the alcove where she'd been working, and his hand immediately sank. He whistled appreciatively.

"How high did you turn the gravity?"

"See you for yourself." She picked up her water bottle and smiled around the mouthpiece when he read the screen.

He turned back to her. "Eight? What, are you planning to retire on Sarigo?"

"Just building up my muscle. You never know when I might have to kick your ass."

Nasim snorted. "If you're training for that, you should be down on the target range. You'll need a gun."

Clare said, "Oh, I can already out-draw you. I'm just getting strong in case I have to finish you off." She swung at his midsection and he jumped back, barely avoiding her fist. He grabbed her forearm and yanked her off-balance, and Clare stumbled. He ducked, wrapped his arms around her waist, and she yelled as he straightened up and swung her head toward the rubber mat of the floor. He looked down at her head from between her knees, her feet dangling in the air as she squirmed to get free.

"Say uncle, Commander."

"You fight dirty, you damn jarhead."

He grinned, and then showed his teeth when Clare's comm went off. "You should answer that, Commander."

She glowered at him, her face turning red as she dangled from his arms. He seemed to strain not at all to hold her as she answered the call. "Commander Cossin."

"This is Captain Hart. Where are you?"

"Just hanging around, Captain. Do you need me?"

"We're coming up on a derelict ship. One of ours. Pick a team and gear up. You're heading over to make sure everything is okay."

She patted Nasim's leg, and he bent forward. She braced one hand on the floor and flipped, wavering a bit when she was upright again. "Understood, sir. We'll be ready for a walk in fifteen." She disconnected and said, "Gear up. We've got an excursion."

His smile faded. "I was going to work out."

Clare put a fist next to her eye and rubbed at imaginary tears, pushing out her bottom lip as she walked past him.

"Next time I'll drop you on your head!" A moment later he added, "Ma'am."

She spun around and walked backwards into the locker room. "If you were wondering what I'd have done in that situation for real? I want you to think real hard about where my head was dangling." She leaned forward and then slammed her head backward, and Nasim cringed and moved both hands to cover his midsection.

She turned her back to him again and peeled off her sweaty shirt. "Fifteen minutes, Gunny. Don't be the one who holds us up."

V. LOST SOULS

Terepians are a highly secretive amphibious people who ratified membership in the Peaceful Sea following the near-cataclysm suffered by their planet during the ACRA Attrition of '19. Generally humanoid in appearance, the Terepians stand out due to the green tint to their skin and the ovoid pupil in their eyes. They are extremely private people. Rather than share information even as basic as their name is against their belief system. They therefore choose Earth words to serve as identification when dealing with outsiders. The reason behind their choices are kept as private as anything else they do.

-- Terepian entry from children's encyclopedia *The Universe and You! Aliens Aea to Zzhe*

Peaceful Sea Vessel *Prospekt* remained silent on their approach despite countless attempts to contact them. Communications Officer Kira Gray hailed them the standard five times requesting an Identity Establishing Code. Without the IDEC, they were forced to rely on Navigator Quimby reading the name off the side of the vessel. Kira confirmed the vessel had been missing for almost fifteen months.

Clare couldn't stop herself from thinking of another vessel that had been missing for nearly that long. She and the rest of her team suited up together in the airlock, wearing the standard gray trousers and sleeveless shirts underneath the baggy dirt-brown EVO suits. Their Fore-Arms weapon platforms were attached outside the suit sleeve, and Clare slipped her hand around the grip. It was activated by squeezing, and it freed them from having to carry bulky weapons everywhere they went.

Nasim was over the disappointment of missing gym time, if he'd ever been truly put-out. The chance of checking out a true ghost vessel was too good for any of them to pass up. Three lieutenants from Security were also accompanying them: Declan Hass, Tomas Green, and a male Terepian called Articulate Right. They waited until they got confirmation the ship was oriented properly and the hatches were locked before they put on their helmets. The blank screens on the front of their helmets flickered as the cameras situated within activated and replaced the emptiness with a three-dimensional holographic representation of the wearer's head.

"Hass, you have a chrome dome," Clare said.

He reached up and touched the control on the side of his helmet. "Shit. Hold on." The image flickered and then he looked at her. "Better?"

"Well, I can see your face. I wouldn't call that an improvement." She winked at him and turned on the communicator on her chest plate. "Kira, you read me, sweetheart?"

"Readings five by five, Commander. You're all set. Life support on the *Prospekt* is nil; we're reading zero life signs. You should be all by yourself over there."

"You're going to have to keep me company, cutie."

"I'd never let you get lonely, Commander."

Clare nodded for Green to open the hatch, and the air pushed past them to enter the vacuum of the umbilical connecting the ships. Clare checked her watch and nodded when the pressure was equalized. They stepped through and made the three-quarter mile trek to the opposite end. Green used a bypass code to open the hatchway to the other ship, and within minutes they were in an airlock that mirrored the one they had just left. They took a moment to adjust the magnetic levels on their boot soles before continuing on at a normal pace.

Hass and Nasim led the way into the corridor, motioning that it was safe to continue. Clare swept the hall with her right arm, keeping the left at her side. The lights mounted on their weapons platforms danced in oddly skewed patterns on the wall. Everything was pristine, as if the ship had just been inspected and cleared for further duty. She touched the filter reading on her suit and frowned at it. "This place is clean. Really, really clean."

"Some people believe in housekeeping, Commander," Nasim said.

"Foreign concept." She turned to the lieutenants. "Articulate, Hass... go down and check the armory. See if they have any guns we can pilfer. Green, check the lifeboats. They couldn't have gotten an entire crew into the shuttles, but maybe the survivors launched. Nasim, you and I are going to check the bridge."

"How come I have to hang out with the boss?"

"So I can keep my eye on you. Come on."

They split up. The lifts were, of course, off-line, so they used the ladders to ascend from one level to the other. As they climbed out of the access port, Nasim smiled at her.

"You know what this reminds me of?"

"The ship we live on? The one that is identical to this one in almost every way?"

"No."

"Of course not. What does it remind you of?"

Nasim dropped his voice and masked his accent to sound like the foreboding Voice of the Night who broadcast horror stories over the broadwave. "The Ghost of the Cosmos."

"Oh, God," Clare groaned. "I can't believe you listen to that crap. I figured you were more of a Zhenhua Je kind of guy."

"Zhenhua is good, if you want a little smut mixed with your horror. He gives me weird nightmares, though. Alien monsters eat my face and tear me limb from limb, but I kind of like it."

Clare laughed. "Does your girlfriend know what crap you fill your mind with?"

"She's the one who got me hooked. And she likes Zhenhua, too."

"Well, she's dating you. Stands to reason she's a freak."

They were moving from doorway to doorway along the corridor, sweeping the rooms with their platforms before moving on. Everything was in its proper place. Nothing seemed to have been touched. Clare was more disturbed by that fact than if the vessel had been ransacked. They reached the bridge and Clare went to the computer monitor near the captain's chair. She plugged in her own power source and, giving it a minute to warm up, brushed her thumb over the screen.

"Damn. I need an authorization code."

Nasim had checked the briefing room and was walking back to

her. "Try the ship's call numbers. Captain Harp said a lot of them did that." He pointed to the plaque on the far wall and walked over to it. He read out the numbers - 87-32-2092 - and Clare punched them in. The screen came to life with a bevy of options.

"Hey, there we go. Captain Stewart Levin. He was an expansive son of a bitch. We have daily updates, plus smaller entries in between." She saved them to her external drive and scrolled down to the bottom to the final message. It was the official captain's log, and she pressed play as Nasim wandered down one of the corridors that branched upward to the Crow's Nest. After a moment, the captain's face filled the screen. Underneath was the date and time.

"*Prospekt* is currently en route to the following coordinates to respond to an unusually truncated distress call. Our communications only picked it up for thirty-eight seconds, but we figure it's better safe than sorry way out here in the middle of nowhere." A faint smile. "I know I'd want someone looking for me."

Clare looked at the empty seat and then scanned the rest of the bridge as he continued speaking. Something was wrong. Something was very wrong, but she couldn't figure out what. Everything was as it should be. Maybe it was that order, that ordinary appearance, that was making the hairs on the back of her neck stand up. She ran her fingers over the grip of her Fore-Arms and looked back at the screen. She watched the captain's image as he spoke, but his words faded as her mind put the pieces together.

Everything was in its place.

Articulate Right interrupted her train of thought. "Eighty lifeboats, accounted for, Commander. No damage."

Nasim returned from the Crow's Nest. "I found some damage. Scratches on the door. Maybe their Navigator isn't as tidy as Anais, huh?"

"They cleaned up after themselves."

Nasim stopped where he was. His smile was nervous as he registered what she was saying. "Oh, come on. Now who's been reading Zhenhua?"

Her heart slammed against her chest, but she wasn't about to panic based on a hunch. "Kira, can you patch me through to Anais, please?"

"Commander? Are you okay?"

"Now. Please." She felt bad for spooking Kira, as she knew she would by being brusque. She saw that the download of files was done, so she took the drive out and secured it in her pocket. Nasim was tense now, watching her from a position near the door.

"Commander?" Anais' voice was high-pitched, innocent, and hearing it calmed Clare just a little. "Kira said you yelled at her. Are you okay?"

"I don't know. Scan the ship again for life signs."

"I've done it twice since you got over there. There are only five."

Clare drummed her hand on her thigh. "Drop the threshold to ten degrees Celsius."

There was a pause and, when Anais spoke again, her voice was thick with dread. "Oh, no. Commander, get out of there."

"How many?"

"I can't even count. They're in the lowest section of the ship. I think they're hibernating. *Commander, get out of there.*" She was almost shrieking now, but it was unnecessary. Nasim beat Clare to the bridge's door by mere seconds, and they were both shouting into their communicators to Green, Hass and Articulate to get back to the hatch as soon as possible. Clare's harsh breathing echoed inside her helmet, and she saw sweat trickling down the back of Nasim's neck as he ran ahead of her. They disconnected the magnets on their boots when they reached the access ladder and used their hands against the wall to propel themselves. It was dizzying, like falling upward, and Nasim helped Clare crawl onto the right level.

"This can't be really happening," he said.

Anais spoke in Clare's ear again. "Oh, God. They're moving..."

Up ahead, Clare saw the three lieutenants waiting at the hatch. She and Nasim waved for them to go back through. They hesitated, but then Hass urged the other two on. They were halfway down the umbilical when Nasim reached the hatch. He turned, and Clare stopped and urged him onward.

"Go on... go!"

"What about you?"

"I'll be right behind you. Believe me."

He hesitated further, but he moved before Clare had to make it an order. Once he was safely through, she scanned the corridor in both directions.

"Where are they coming from, Anais?"

"Your starboard." She sounded close to tears as Clare turned and lifted both arms.

Clare said, "How long?"

"They're moving fast now. They know you're there."

Captain Harp's voice drowned out the last word of Anais'

sentence. "Commander, get your ass off that ship. If this~"

"We need visual confirmation, sir."

She heard the scraping of claws moving along metal surfaces and the sweat under her suit turned ice cold. She swallowed hard and tensed, her hands hovering over the trigger of her Fore-Arms. From the corner of her eye, she saw Nasim waiting for her on the other side of the umbilical. She bared her teeth.

"Come on, you assho~"

The first pale-white creature burst into the corridor so quickly Clare took an instinctive step back. It was a male, with a crest fanning out over its beady black eyes. The bottom of its head spread out in a disgusting diamond shape to reveal the maw underneath. The creature's bony shoulders spread out on either side of its crowned head, spindly arms grasping for purchase on the slick floor. It looked at her and widened its mouth so that she could see its hideous tongue and four sharp teeth. It bent its head down toward the floor, braced its four legs and both arms on the ground, and pounded.

Clare opened fire with both barrels and blew its ugly head off just as three more - two females and another male - emerged from the corridor. Their screech was like needles scraping her eardrums as she continued firing, blowing off parts of them as she stepped over the edge of the hatch. She only stopped shooting to push the door shut, wincing as the creatures slammed against the opposite side while she was securing it.

Panting, Clare turned and ran for the opposite end of the umbilical as fast as her feet could carry her. Nasim was waiting at the terminus, and his arms wrapped around her and lifted her as easily as he had in the gym. He pivoted, dumped her unceremoniously on the airlock floor, and pulled the hatch shut behind her.

In the sudden silence, the away team could only hear their own panting and gasping. Clare lay flat on her back in the middle of the space, tears burning her eyes. She felt like a little girl who had just woken up from a nightmare, but she knew the nightmare was really only beginning. Above her, Nasim's face was a ghastly pasty color and his bottom lip was trembling. If she was a little girl with a nightmare, he was a boy who'd broken a window. The terror in the room was palatable, but none of them could give voice to it for fear of making it really real.

The inner door of the airlock opened and Captain Harp joined them. Nasim snapped his head up and met Harp's gaze.

"Are we away?"

"We're away." Harp was focused on Clare. "Well? You stayed behind to get visual confirmation." He pressed his lips together and forced himself to ask. "Did you get it?"

"Aye, sir." She swallowed hard and forced the words out. "That ship was killed by Harvestmen. They're back."

Hass slumped against the wall and continued until he was lying on the floor in an unconscious heap. Everyone in the room stared at him in stunned silence. Despite everything they had done, despite the hairy situations everyone on the crew had been in, none of them had ever actually seen someone pass out cold from sheer fright before.

VI. HARVESTMEN

"There are two methods to dealing with harvestmen. One is to run as fast as possible in the opposite direction. The other doesn't work. And to be honest, the first one isn't all that effective either."
~ old joke

Captain Harp's crew and Nasim's unit stood at attention along the windows in the observation room. The *Prospekt* hung in the near distance, silent and ominous to those who knew what lurked aboard it. By now word had trickled down through the ranks that the away team had encountered Harvestmen, but whether or not the news was believed depended on the messenger. Some thought it was a sick joke. Others thought someone had just panicked and made a rush judgment.

Anais had to be taken to medical to be sedated. Dr. Monroe assured them she would make a full recovery, but the tension of the moment had been too much for the poor girl. Clare felt bad for exacerbating the situation and made herself a promise she would visit to apologize. They were back in their everyday uniforms, and at Captain Harp's signal, they lifted their right arms in a salute to the ship and its lost crew.

Captain Harp spoke to Sergeant Kite in Weapons. "Fire."

Two missiles streaked from the underside of the *Paralus*, streaking ahead until they impacted the opposite ends of the *Prospekt*'s hull. Clare flinched from the resulting flash and, when she looked, the other vessel and its horrific passengers were gone. The soldiers dropped their arms and Captain Harp stepped away from the windows. The only sound in the room was soft footsteps on the carpet as they took their seats around the horizontal obelisk of their briefing table.

Clare spoke first. She gave a brief recap of what had happened aboard the *Prospekt*, pausing so Articulate and Hass could tell what they had experienced, and then Clare was forced to relive the swarm of Harvestmen she had seen. She had never heard the room so silent. Even during the tensest briefing there was always the click of a pen, the shift of cloth against a seat, or any number of nervous tics or noises. As she described the Harvestman in detail, her skin erupted in gooseflesh and she rolled her shoulders so that her shirt wasn't touching her flesh so obnoxiously.

Articulate said, "ACRA destroyed the last Harvestman nest thirty-two years ago. Their home planet was quarantined. Burnt."

"And yet." Nasim held his hands out helplessly. "I don't want to believe it any more than... hell, I want to believe it less than anyone on this ship. When I was a boy, Harvestmen invaded the colony where my parents were posted. I got put on an extraction trolley, and I got to watch as my father was torn to pieces by one of those things. The thought they somehow survived..." He laughed without humor. "Well. That's just the thing, though. We don't want to believe it because it's so horrible. But things like that are too horrible to die easy. It makes all the sense in the universe that they're back."

Harp said, "We can't just sit around and hope that this nest was the only one left. We need to put our other commissions on hold and figure out where they got aboard the *Prospekt*. If there's a breeding ground out there, our duty is to find it. Commander, you got the captain's log?"

She nodded. "Kira is going over them now. They were en route to respond to a strange distress call that cut off after a few seconds. I think the log doesn't show anything worth investigating, we should follow up on that."

Harp nodded. "I'll have Kira send a wave to Base and let them know we're taking a detour. But no one is to mention Harvestmen in any official communication. We're keeping it aboard the ship until we know how big this threat is. No sense in causing a widespread panic."

Kalliste Monroe, the ship's physician, looked down at her folded hands and spoke softly. "With all due respect, Captain? That may be precisely what the crew of the *Prospekt* thought. We should ensure that people know about this no matter what the outcome of our search is. If the Harvestmen overtake us, we owe it to the next ship to warn them."

"You have a point, Doctor. I'll have Kira prepare a message that we'll send out if... it becomes necessary. We'll warn any other ships to keep a wide berth and blow us out of the sky if it comes to that."

Nasim said, "We should also prepare countermeasures in case the Harvestmen do overtake us. We know how they act. After they... take the ship... they'll burrow down and wait for the next victim to blunder across them. We can find the places they'd be most likely to hide and lay traps for them."

"Have your men get that done. Good thinking, all of you. Commander, staying behind for a visual was reckless. But now that the ship is gone, it would have been far too easy to ignore the readings as anomalies or glitches. You did the right thing."

"Thank you, sir."

He dismissed them until they had anything more concrete to go on, and Clare caught up with Dr. Monroe at the door. "Excuse me, Kali. Do you think it would be okay if I visited Anais in the infirmary?"

"I was going to ask you to, but I didn't want to put you on the spot. She was asking for you when we sedated her. Wouldn't let us hypo her until she was assured you made it out in one piece. She'll be awake in about twenty minutes."

Clare smiled through her guilt. "Thanks."

Nasim caught up with her at the lift. He rubbed his thumb over his top lip, eyes cast downward, and remained silent until they were safely closed inside the car.

"Listen, Clare. About... leaving you behind..."

"When?"

He stared at her. "On the *ship*. I... I ran away"

"I don't recall it that way, Gunny. I recall a stubborn-ass Marine actually following my order to get his ass to safety. I'm thinking of commemorating it with a holiday. I may write a children's book and call it The Day a Marine Listened to a Lowly Commander."

"Bite me, ma'am." He folded his hands in front of his waist and watched the numbers rise. Finally he said, "Glad you're okay."

"Thanks."

He grinned and shook her head. "I'm just jealous you were the one who stayed behind."

"Did I offend your masculinity?"

"Hell no. I'm confident enough in my manhood that I can run away and scream like a little girl." She laughed as the lift doors opened. "Nah, I'm just pissed. You faced down four Harvestmen by yourself. With that story, you're never going to have to pay a drink for as long as you live."

She waved goodbye to him and rode the lift back to her quarters. She preempted Pam's standard greeting by speaking first. "Lights low, Pam. And play something soft. Quiet." She walked down the corridor to her bathroom, knelt in front of the toilet, and threw up. The sight of Harvestmen barreling down the corridor toward her, their jaws wide, slavering for a feast, had twisted her stomach in knots but she refused to let it control her. She hadn't been alone for a minute since returning from the ship, and she could only now face the fear and horror.

The first reference to the Harvestmen was in the diary of an alien explorer who had died while humans still considered the oceans of Earth to be treacherous. He claimed to have seen them on a planet with landmasses covered by grasslands, the scythes on their arms sweeping in a delicate ballet and slicing the stalks down. He said they had lifted their heads to follow the track of his ship, and he dismissed them as little more than beasts of burden. When he and his team landed, the Harvestmen approached the ship in an eager rush.

Eight members of the explorer's team were devoured before he managed to take off, incinerating a handful of the creatures that clung to the exterior of the ship as he escaped.

Daring men with more bullets than brains took this report as a challenge and began searching for the planet, seeing it as a pristine hunting ground with the ultimate game. Hunters who found the planet rarely returned, and those who managed it were changed. Many of them never picked up a gun again. Some claimed the Harvestmen were able to speak to your mind, make you do things, make you open doors to let them in.

After a century, reports began surfacing of Harvestmen on other planets and it became apparent they had found a way off their isolated home. Travel to the world that had never been granted a name was forbidden, and the solar system was declared No Passage. Harvestmen, once seen as mindless agrarian beasts, proved themselves to be crafty adversaries. They passed up opportunities to feed in exchange for slipping unnoticed onto ships.

Within five hundred years, Harvestmen had managed to spread across most of the civilized spiral without building a single ship of their own.

ACRA made it their mission to wipe the beasts out. Unfortunately as the Harvestmen had no true homeland and no ships of their own, the collateral damage to other worlds quickly became astounding. ACRA vessels destroyed entire fleets to kill one nest of Harvestmen. For every Harvestman ACRA killed, there were hundreds of civilians who paid the price. But the Harvestmen continued to thrive, and they became even more vicious in response to the attacks. Soon other planets were signing up to join ACRA just so they could assist.

Thus began the ACRA Attritions. For ten years, the alliance chased Harvestmen from one planet to the next. Solar systems were annexed. Planets were carpet-bombed. People were relocated from their homelands in order to create "roach motels" for the beasts.

After two decades of constant warfare, ACRA announced that the final Harvestman had been slaughtered. Carapaces were hung on the walls of every ACRA building near and far. Most of the displaced people were allowed to return to their home planets (although some of them became ACRA property, but the alliance was more than happy to rent the land back to them).

Clare leaned back against the cold wall of her bathroom and rubbed her face. They couldn't be back. Harvestmen couldn't be back, it just wasn't fair. She stood up carefully, did a quick review of her body to make sure she was finished throwing up, and splashed her face with cold water. She raked her fingers through her hair until it stood up in short spikes, then left her quarters. Anais would be awake, and Clare desperately needed to spend some time looking at something pretty.

VII. THERAPY

"Hey, Joe."
"Oh, hi, Ryan. Hey, are you buying birth control pills for your wife or something?"
"(laughs) No! I'm buying Testost. For me!"
"Testost? What the heck is that?"
"It's a thrice-a-year pill for men!"
"Birth control for men? You're pulling my leg, buddy."
"Not at all! And Testost is not just birth control. It also protects against sexual transmitted diseases."
"Wow. I'll bet it's pretty expensive."
"Worth every penny, but it's not coming out of your pocket! Testost is covered by most health-care plans."
"Sounds amazing! Say, where do they stock it in this store...?"
"TESTOST. Use as directed."
- broadwave advertisement.

Lieutenant Declan Hass stood under the overhead shower spout and let the steaming water pour over his head and down his back. The shower stalls were white tile booths, with narrow windows at eye level so visibility wasn't compromised. He swept his hand over his face, clearing the water from his eyes. Radka Saric was showering in the next row of stalls, and she looked over when she felt him watching her.

"You okay, Dec?"

He nodded slowly. Everyone had been asking him that, and he could only assume everyone else on the away team was getting the same treatment. They were the first people of the current generation to have encountered real live Harvestmen. She turned to one side to continue scrubbing off, and Declan turned his back to her. In doing so, he saw Sadiq Malki in the stall beside him. His dark skin glistened, and his curls were flattened against his head. He had been looking at Declan, but he looked away quickly.

The three of them showered in silence until Radka turned off her stall and wrapped a towel around her body to leave. Declan watched her, not bothering to turn around when he heard the stall door open behind him. Sadiq stepped into the stall and closed the door behind him, and Declan braced his hands against the pass-through in front of him as Sadiq touched his hip.

"You really okay?" Sadiq asked softly.

"I'm fine." He dropped one hand and covered Sadiq's. He turned to look at the engineer over his shoulder, and closed his eyes as Sadiq leaned down to kiss his shoulder. He guided Sadiq's hand forward and stepped back until their bodies met. He let his weight rest against Sadiq's and his voice softened. "Better now, though."

Sadiq moved his lips to Declan's neck. "Yeah?" He looped his fingers around Declan's penis, moving his other hand to cradle the balls in the palm of his hand. "Want me to make it better?"

"If you can."

"I'll do my best."

Sadiq moved his hand slowly, pressing against the curve of Declan's ass. Declan felt Sadiq's erection swelling against him and reached back, sliding his hand over his partner's hip. The water poured over them, over Sadiq's chest and down Declan's back, and soon they were both breathing heavily. Sadiq circled the head of Declan's cock with his palm and Declan groaned. He opened his eyes at the sound of movement in one of the other stalls, and caught a brief glimpse of Dr. Monroe pulling the privacy curtain.

It wouldn't be the first time they'd had an audience, and he had turned a blind eye to other such couplings, so he wasn't terribly worried about the good doctor's sensibilities. He hoped she enjoyed the show. He pressed back against the sharp angles of Sadiq's hips and moved his legs farther apart. His hand moved from Sadiq's side to his cock, squeezing the shaft before guiding it between his legs.

"I'm up to date on my pill," Sadiq murmured against the back of Declan's neck.

Declan wasn't worrying about disease transmission, but he was grateful Sadiq was current. He hated the barriers, and he wasn't going to suggest they stop just so they could put one on. Sadiq pressed insistently against him and, after teasing him for a moment, Sadiq moaned and pressed inside. Declan groaned with pleasure and rolled his head back as Sadiq continued kissing his neck and shoulder. He squeezed Declan's balls and ran his fingers along the length of his lover's cock using the pouring water as lubrication.

Declan groaned and rolled his head forward as he came, watching the white ribbons of come hit the tile before being washed away almost immediately by the shower. He leaned forward and gripped the wall with both hands, pressing back as Sadiq began to thrust against him with more force. His fingers dug into Declan's hips as he arched his back and came. He moved his hand to the middle of Declan's back, stroking upward along his spine until Declan straightened and twisted to kiss Sadiq.

They parted, and Declan held his hands under the water before washing Sadiq's cock. Sadiq closed his eyes and swayed and then said, "You off-duty?"

"Yeah. I was going to grab a bite to eat."

"I think I'll join you."

Declan turned off the shower and they stepped out to wrap themselves in towels. As they passed Dr. Monroe's stall, she called out, "I'm disappointed, boys. No cuddling?"

Declan put his arm across Sadiq's shoulders. "Gotta save something for the six o'clock show, Doc. Get your tickets early."

Anais was sitting up in her infirmary bed, legs crossed under the blankets, and she held her hands palm-up on the stretched material. Thetis, sitting on the foot of the bed, spilled five drops of honey-colored liquid onto each palm, then used her thumbs to massage it into the skin. She used long, sweeping arcs so that soon the entire hand save the fingers was glistening. Anais tried to hold back her giggle and hunched her shoulders. "It tickles."

"That means it's working," Thetis said softly. "Do you smell that?"

Anais closed her eyes and breathed deeply. "Mm. I do. What is that?"

"It's the fragrance of a rare bloom on my planet. The scent of it is said to speed healing of mental scars."

She smiled and opened her eyes. "Thank you." She saw movement behind Thetis and her smile widened. "Commander."

Thetis turned and saw Rani Clare Cossin in the doorway. "Hello, Commander."

"Hi. Am I interrupting?"

"Not at all. I was merely applying a folk cure from Leucothea. I heard of the poor Navigator's collapse and I know the Peaceful Sea doesn't pride itself on being a family-oriented organization. I wasn't sure she would have anyone to visit her. Dr. Monroe said it would be all right, and the young lady agreed to see me." She smiled at Anais. "We've become fast friends."

Anais nodded. "She didn't even mind that I embarrassed myself when she first came in."

"You did not. You merely commented on the color of my skin."

Anais sheepishly explained, "I blurted out that I didn't mind talking with her because blue is my favorite color."

Clare shrugged and moved closer to the bed. "Skin color was a big deal in our society for a long time. We're a little more sensitive about it than other races. I could come back~"

Anais and Thetis both refused. Thetis unfolded her long legs and slid off the edge of the mattress. She smoothed down her gowns. "I have taken up too much of her time as it is. I will return later." She looked at Anais. "Try not to wash them for at least an hour so it can fully penetrate the skin. If applied properly, the scent will linger for over a day. It should act as a calming influence."

"Thank you."

Thetis dipped her chin to her, then did the same to Clare before leaving the women alone. She lingered at the doorway and listened to their voices drift from across the curtain.

"Here, smell."

"Wow. What is that?"

"A Leucothean flower." Anais sniffed deeply again. "It's amazing. I may trade her for a bottle of it."

Thetis smiled as she heard Clare sit on the edge of the bed. "You may need it. I heard you were worried about me today."

"No. Not really. I mean..." Anais sighed. "My father told me horror stories about the Harvestmen. And when I thought about you, I mean all of you guys trapped on the ship with them, I guess I panicked. I kind of made a fool of myself, huh?"

"Are you kidding? I came here to thank you. You saved my life,

Anais."

"Oh, come on."

"No, I'm serious. You told me where they were, told me when they were coming. You got me and my team out of there in one piece. I owe you, chick."

Anais sniffled, and Thetis heard Clare move closer to her. There was a rustling of clothes, obviously a hug, and then Anais' spoke in a muffled voice.

"I'm glad you're okay."

"Back at you. When you get out of here, I'll treat you to a nice dinner in the commissary."

"I'd like that."

The women continued their conversation, but Thetis was aware she had already overstayed her welcome. She covered her hair with her robe's hood and slipped quietly out of the infirmary.

VIII. LISTEN

Following the attacks of Earth colonies that left hundreds of thousands of human expatriates dead, the juvenile survivors were quickly gathered like fallen leaves and distributed to any willing home. They found shelter in group homes until they could be placed permanently. The idea of a 'nuclear family' of parents and two or four biological children became a quaint idea of a distant past. Children grew up with siblings of a different species, and family acquired a completely new definition seemingly overnight. Some say it was this melting pot that led to the accords allowed alien species to join ACRA and Peaceful Sea and the British Rule in numbers never before seen.
~ Enlightened by the Silver Lining, by Pope Evaristus V

A web of four crossed metal braces covered Kira Gray's short blue-black hair, stretching down under the back collar of her uniform to a power pack mounted between her shoulders. Those unfamiliar with the Op'tra people assumed the objects protruding from either side of her head served as speakers she used as the ship's communications officer. The filters actually deafened her to a large degree, silencing the cacophony of boots on metal platforms, inhalations and exhalations, heartbeats, digestion growls, squeaks and squawks and grunts and groans the humans around her made without even realizing.

Despite the mufflers, her hearing was considered extraordinarily acute by the fellow members of the crew. Her white hand, three-fingered with two dexterous thumbs on either side, rested on her console and she tilted her head to the side. A long step of someone who weighed... a particular amount... and stood five and a half feet approached her station. She could hear the approach echoing off the contoured walls of the ship's bridge and turned toward Clare before she had officially announced her presence.

"Commander. You were taking longer strides. You were trying to trick me."

"You caught me. How do you always know?"

Kira shrugged. "How do you recognize someone who is wearing an unusual outfit? You changed one note of yourself, but the symphony was the same. You sound beautiful as ever, Commander."

Clare smiled at Kira's expressionless face. The Op'tra were known to give nightmares to the uninitiated due to their lack of eyes. It was a wrongness, a blankness, that screwed with people's minds even more than the fact Op'tra people weren't born to a specific gender. To Clare, Kira was a beautiful woman with a tiny nose and a small mouth. Her head was smooth from the bridge of her nose to the hairline, but Clare still focused where the eyes should have been when she spoke.

"You said you had something for us? From the logs of the *Prospekt*?"

"I do. I apologize for taking so long, but there was quite a lot to go through."

She turned back to her station and ran her fingers over the console. They had left behind the *Prospekt*'s final resting place a week earlier, and the crew was eager to get underway. Clare understood their anxiety, but she didn't want to dash off on a wild goose chase only to lose time backtracking when they found more concrete evidence.

"We're fortunate the captain was so talkative. He often ran low on topics and simply reiterated their current mission, including destinations. What he didn't say, I was able to pick up from the ambient conversations in the room while he was recording. I've sent the codes to Navigation, and we've laid in a course that will follow their path as exactly as we can manage. If the Harvestmen came from a passing ship or something they unexpectedly encountered on the journey, I can't promise we'll have the same luck." She rubbed her thumbs together. "If you can call that luck."

"I don't." Clare examined the three-dimensional chart projected above Kira's station. A pulsing yellow line connected the dots of locations where the *Prospekt* had stopped for any length of time during their fateful final voyage. "Is one of these showing the coordinates of the distress call they were following? I think it was a Harvestmen trap. Seeing if they could draw someone in."

"It's a strong theory. It sounds like something they would do, and it would account for the brevity of the signal. The coordinates of the distress call is the farthest in the *Prospekt*'s log, so it will be the one we reach last." She gestured vaguely to the right side of the map which, of course, she couldn't directly reference. It was only there for Clare's benefit.

"Okay. How long should it take to cover all these places?"

"There are seven locations. Giving ourselves time to check each one for the potential of being the source of the Harvestmen and light-plus travel to each one, we'll reach the distress call's origin in six days."

It would have to do. Clare thanked her and left the bridge. Six days wasn't a terrible length of time to chase down a lead, but the star map showed them going in the completely wrong direction to fulfill another commission. She stopped at one of the computer terminals in the corridor and activated it with her palm. "Computer, location of ship's guest Thetis:scholar."

Thetis was in her assigned quarters curled in one of the spacious armchairs with her bare feet tucked underneath her. She responded to the chime and put her book aside as Clare stepped inside. Thetis smiled and stood, bowing forward with her hands on her hips in deference to the Commander's rank. "What a surprise. Welcome to my humble rooms."

"Not so humble anymore. You've redecorated." She ran her eyes along the gold-hemmed black cloth that hung over the walls, pausing at the basins full of water that had been mounted on the wall at mid-chest level. "I like it. Looks, ah... serene. Very pretty. I hope I'm not interrupting anything."

"No. I was simply enjoying one of the novels from the ship's library. Your literature is amazing. Leucotheans never thought of scribing fictional tales, but I find them amazing. So many of them feel real, the characters and the stories. I am very impressed by the Fourth Epoch writing, but there was genius even in the First Epoch, before~"

Clare waved a hand. "Whoa. You haven't even been aboard the ship for a week. How many books have you read?"

"One hundred and eighty-four."

"Wow. I don't think I've read a hundred books in my entire life. Even if you count textbooks."

"You don't read?" She seemed shocked by the idea.

"I... there's..." She shifted uncomfortably. "I like books, and stories, but I never got the knack of reading them to myself."

"Who read them to you?"

Clare had grasped the easy topic of conversation to save herself from the harder news, but she found herself mired in dangerous territory. Her mind produced an image of a tall brunette made even taller by standing on a box, lit from below by a flashlight, sweeping a cape made from her sheet as Clare laughed with delight. She shook her head and the image faded.

Thetis had picked up her book and was smiling at the cover. "I seem to enjoy it very much."

"Well, the bound literature in the library doesn't get a lot of traffic. Most people prefer to use their tablets. It's easier that way. I'm sure you can take as many as you want. And keep them for a while, too. You might want to take your time with one. Really absorb it."

Thetis nodded slowly. "Yes. Well. Surely I won't be gracing your vessel for long enough to become a nuisance to the other literates aboard."

"That's what I came to discuss with you. The situation with the Harvestmen has taken precedence. We've got to do everything we can to find out where this nest came from, and that's going to mean going the wrong direction for nearly a week. We'll be able to cut across and take a more up-north route to get you to your people, but we're going to be drastically delayed. We've already lost a week, and it looks like we're going to lose even more. We'd arrange for you to transfer to another ship, but this far out, it's highly unlikely anyone is going to swing over. I'm sorry, Thetis, but it looks like you'll have to stay with us a bit longer than you planned."

Thetis' smile had faded, but she looked resigned to the facts. "Then my Regent will simply have to wait. The important thing is that you arrived on Leucothea and retrieved me in time. I was not particularly looking forward to our new homeland, so I'm more than happy to bide my time aboard your vessel. With your books."

Clare nodded. "Thanks for understanding. The delay is our fault, so your Regent won't be charged for the extra time. We'll let him know about it all during our next wide-wave."

"Actually, Commander, I would like to be the one to break the news. It will serve the dual purpose of informing him of the change and allowing him to see I'm not being held against my will." She smiled and shrugged. "He can be paranoid."

"Right. I'll let you get back to your book."

"Commander?" She stopped at the door and turned back. "Why did you tell me?"

Clare furrowed her brow and smiled. "Well, we figured you'd eventually notice you were still aboard the ship instead of where we were taking you."

"No, why did *you* tell me? Surely this duty doesn't fall under the auspices of your rank."

"Oh. I don't know." She touched her hair just above her ear. "You went to see Anais when she was in the infirmary. You didn't have to do that. And I thought you should hear it from me and not some lieutenant you haven't met."

Thetis nodded. "I thank you, Commander. It was appreciated."

"Sure."

"I would also like to extend an invitation, if it isn't out of place. Your ordeal aboard the *Prospekt...* I've noticed those members who were aboard the ship when the Harvestmen attacked have been visiting the infirmary for sleep aids. I realize that you are in an awkward situation. Everyone aboard this ship is either below you in rank, or your superior officer. There is no one you can admit your fears to. But if you hold them to yourself, you risk allowing them to fester. I would like to offer myself as a... confessor. It doesn't have to be religious if you don't desire, but while I am here, I am willing to help you bear the weight."

Clare looked stunned, but she finally nodded. "All right. I may take you up on that. Thanks. I'll see you around the ship, Thetis:scholar."

Thetis waited until the doors closed before she regained her seat, running her fingers over the artful cover of the book. The Regent would just have to cope with her absence; she could think of worse places to be. She thumbed through the book until she found the place she had stopped reading and resumed the story. She was discovering methods and tricks that authors seemed to favor throughout the centuries and across genres. She was particularly fond of devastating twists in the plot. She could never anticipate them but, in retrospect, they often seemed inevitable.

Kira separated the audio of the recordings into distinct tracks, isolating them and buffing each track until it was as audible to the humans in the room as it was to her. She played them in the briefing room with the command staff present, as well as Nasim Senech to represent the Marines aboard the ship.

Kira said, "There remains no record from the discovery of the distress call's origin, and there are no recordings made afterward despite the fact the *Prospekt* had to get from there to where we found it. Even if they didn't stop, it would have taken them three days, and I don't see their captain remaining silent for that long."

Captain Harp said, "You determined the name of the vessel they were seeking?"

"Aye, sir. The snippet of distress call was eventually decoded, and their communications officer was able to dig through the noise to find the IDEC of the ship." She touched the raised pips on her tablet to refresh her memory. "The ship that sent the truncated distress signal was the PSV *Juno*."

Clare started as if someone had kicked her chair. She looked at Kira and softly said, "Say again?"

"The PSV *Juno*. Missing for two years, which is just a few months longer than the *Prospekt* has been derelict. The last transmission from the *Juno* was~"

Clare cut her off. "Yeah, I know when the last transmission from the *Juno* was sent. I..." She realized everyone at the table was staring at her, and Kira looked stunned.

"Commander, your vital signs are increasing to dangerous levels."

Captain Harp said, "Commander? What's wrong?"

Clare's hands were shaking. "The *Juno*, sir. That's my..." She swallowed hard and closed her eyes. "Laikyn was stationed aboard the *Juno* when it went missing."

CHAPTER THREE

IX. GRIEVING

Prescott, Laikyn (Lieutenant Colonel). Marine, Linguist Division. (28). Born in Maioset Province Colony. A decorated linguist, awarded for her vast knowledge of languages. Fully conversant in six original Earth languages, seventeen xenodialects, and a capable translator in fourteen more. She is survived by her sister.
~ obituary, two years old

The confirmation of the distressed ship's identity, combined with his first officer's connection to the vessel, prompted Captain Harp to suggest a change in tactics. Rather than retracing the *Prospekt*'s route, they would immediately set a course for the *Juno*. The fact the scuttled vessel had an encounter with another missing PSV ship indicated a connection that couldn't be denied. He had Anais set a new bearing and dismissed the command crew. He asked Clare to hold back and spoke only when they were alone in the briefing room.

"Will you be okay with this, Commander? I can order you to take some downtime."

"No, sir. I've spent too long wondering. I can't sit out when I finally have a chance to know the truth. No matter how bad it is."

Harp nodded. "Let me know if that changes."

"Aye, sir."

"We'll reach the coordinates of the distress call in two days. If you're not going to take downtime for the search, then I suggest you take it easy until we arrive. Understood?"

She nodded. "I'll do my best."

She left the briefing room ahead of him, finally letting her mind reel at the idea of finally knowing what had happened to Laikyn. Over the past two years she had forced herself to come up with countless horrific scenarios just to prepare herself for the worst. She knew that if she thought up terrible scenarios for Laikyn's disappearance then whatever the truth was, no matter how bad, would pale in comparison. But "killed by Harvestmen" hadn't even been an option. She entered the lift and pressed her shoulders against the far wall, slumping with her arms across her stomach as she let the car carry her through the ship to the Home level.

She let herself in, ignoring Pam's greeting as she went directly to the news article she had printed out and saved so Laikyn could have a good laugh at it when they found her. She could practically hear Laikyn laughing, her eyes wide with horror and fascination as she read the small inked words.

"Oh, my God, you saved it?"

"Well, sure. How often do you get to read your own obituary?"

Laikyn's name was relatively high in the very long article, due to her rank and position on the vessel. She found it with ease, as if the section was written in glowing letters. She had it memorized, but something about actually reading the words comforted her mind. She touched the last line of the obituary and her eyes filled with tears.

When she finally put the printout back into the drawer, she knew where she had to go. She took off her jerkin and replaced it with a casual jacket to look less official, then put her Capture device in her pocket. She didn't know why she was taking it, but a part of her brain insisted she have it with her wherever she was going. She left her quarters and wandered the Home level, mind racing with disjointed memories of Laikyn - a hand, hair whipping in the wind, a pencil threaded between three fingers snapping - until she realized where she was headed.

Clare stood outside the temporary rooms Thetis had been given and, after a moment, pressed the call button.

Thetis answered less than a minute after Clare's presence was announced by the Pam, and she smiled warmly. "Hello, Commander."

"Hi. I was wondering if you had any of the... that oil you gave to Anais when she was in the infirmary. I think you said it helped mental scars, so, uh..."

"Of course. Please, come inside." She left the door open when she walked away, giving Clare little choice but to follow her. The main room was lit by candles beside the bed and along the dresser.

Clare noticed the blankets were disturbed. "Oh. I hope you weren't sleeping."

"I was. It's okay." She closed a drawer and carried over a small teardrop shaped bottle. "Leucotheans have a polyphasic sleep cycle, and I was nearing my next wakeful period anyway. Here." She placed the bottle in Clare's hand, then covered it with her own. "I can assist you in applying it if you wish. It's dependent on what you wish to accomplish."

Clare looked at Thetis' hands and the honey-colored liquid in the jar. "You said I could talk to you if I wanted, right? About anything."

"Yes, of course."

"Is now good for you?"

Thetis nodded. "We can go somewhere you might find more comfortable, if you like. The aesthetics of this room are better suited to a Leucothean."

"I wasn't going to say anything. But yeah, we should be able to find someplace."

Thetis smiled. "I actually had a location in mind."

The arboretum was empty this time of day, although Clare paused at the terminal to ensure Articulate Right wasn't occupying one of the tide pools. She explained to Thetis that he was a Terepian, and she smiled. "Oh, I am well aware of Terepians and their affinity for the water. Our world was a very desirable vacation spot for their people." She gestured with one hand, the sleeve of her robe billowing around her wrist as she moved. "I've found a nice spot over here where we can be undisturbed."

The pool Thetis led her to was enclosed in a waist-high stone wall. Clare sat and removed the Capture from her pocket, and Thetis sat quietly beside her and waited for Clare to break the silence. Finally, Clare began to explain about the *Prospekt's* annihilation and the connection it had to the missing *Juno*. She opened the Capture device and scrolled to a still image of Laikyn. She was facing the camera, lips pressed together in a stifled smile. Her eyes were wide, and her hands were laced behind her back as she mugged for the photographer.

Thetis let Clare look in silence for a long moment before she softly inquired, "Who is she?"

Clare traced the lines of Laikyn's face. "She's my sister. My lover."

A line appeared between Thetis' eyebrows. "That romantic union would not be shunned by your people?"

"She wasn't my birth sister. We were both orphaned in the same attack twenty years ago."

"These Harvestmen...?"

"No, this was just after the Harvestmen annihilation. Some people were not happy with how ACRA handled the war. Too many casualties and collateral damage, too little reward. We were killing our own people to take out a handful of Harvestmen, and the fuckers were still coming on just as strong. So this group decided they wanted to go to war against ACRA. They started bombing our colonies. They hit one with a biological bomb that targeted people with a certain blood type. They were trying to show ACRA how to do precision strikes."

Thetis shook her head. "What a horrible cycle."

Clare laughed. "You don't see the wisdom in killing a bunch of civilians to protest the death of civilians? You're obviously not military." She sniffled. "Fortunately they only hit the business centers. Schools were on the other side of town, so most of the children survived no matter what their blood type was. Of course that meant that, in one moment, the orphan population jumped by about a hundred percent.

"I was eight and Laikyn was ten. We stayed in this little holding area for a while. I don't know how long, but I have distinct memories of different seasons. At least two summers. We finally got moved to this house that was just full of lost children from the attack. We were the littlest ones, so we got a little room underneath the stairs. It was just big enough for two beds. People thought we were twins, because she was small for her age and we had sort of the same hair.

"She could read, and I couldn't. So she would read books during the day, and at night she would act them out for me. She did voices and she stomped around on our mattresses like monsters or spies.

Sometimes I got to play roles, and she would whisper in my ear what I had to do. Even when I learned how to read, I didn't have any interest in reading a book by myself. I would just give them to Laikyn. When we got older, the books started to have romantic scenes. She would be the dashing hero and I'd be the damsel, so she would sweep me up in her arms and kiss my lips and cheeks and eyes."

She smiled and closed her eyes. "Sometimes we would dance. Neither of us knew how to dance, of course, so we would just hold each other and sort of... sway." She mimicked the movement with her hand, then chuckled. "When we got old enough to be moved into separate rooms, Laikyn would crawl into bed with me because she couldn't sleep alone. She had a huge bed all to herself, an entire room with no one but her, but she needed me pressed up against her to fall asleep. I didn't mind. I liked holding her. After that, we got old enough that sleeping in the same bed offered... opportunities."

Thetis smiled. "You loved each other your whole lives."

"Yeah." Clare's voice was barely audible. "When we slept under the stairs, every morning the Matron would come down early to start breakfast for all of us. She wasn't a small woman, and her every step was like thunder booming over our heads. It woke us up every morning, and we were *always* afraid until we remembered. It never occurred to us to just plug our ears. As scary as those first moments were, comforting each other afterward made it worth the fright."

Thetis put her hand on Clare's shoulder and then moved it to her neck. "I am sorry."

Clare reached up, not unkindly, and moved Thetis' hand away. "Thank you."

Thetis folded her hands in her lap. Clare leaned forward, elbows on her knees, and appreciated the silence.

X. SALVE

Leucothea is a water planet, with ninety-two percent of its surface covered by lakes and oceans. The relatively minor landmasses have been heavily industrialized in order to support the Leucothean people. Against these odds, a large landmass in the planet's southern hemisphere is host to abundant plant life. The flowers of this continent (Euxine, as it is known to the inhabitants) have been shown to have abundant healing properties when combined with the low-level psychic ability shown by Leucotheans. There is little to support the claim that the lotions are merely placebos, and the true healing is done psychically by the Leucothean administering it to the patient.
~ Health & Healing in the Universe: What Works, What to Avoid, and How to Stay Alive in Alien Environments · Volume 5, by Dr. Kalliste Monroe

Thetis removed the stopper from the bottle and held it under her nose, inhaling the scent with her eyes closed. "The technique will be different than it was with Anais. Your heart is hurting, so it will require a slightly stronger methodology. I must warn you that it may open wounds..."

"The wounds are there. If it'll help..." She folded her fingers in a 'bring it on' gesture.

Thetis nodded and moistened her fingers with the oils. "Think of a moment in which you were angry with Laikyn."

Clare frowned. "Angry?"

"Love is strong because it is slowly kindled. It grows and it's nourished. But anger comes in a flash. It consumes you wholly in a single instant. The emotion required for this to work needs to be strong, so anger works best. Just think of a single moment when you and Laikyn perhaps did not agree with one another."

Clare closed her eyes and thought back. It wasn't hard to think of fights; she and Laikyn had their share of disagreements. But they were typical fights between people who had spent their lives together. Issues of space, borrowed clothing, messes not cleaned up, but nothing really huge. She had been annoyed with Laikyn on a regular basis, but angry? She couldn't think of a time when she had been really, truly...

Oh.

There was *that*.

Clare opened her eyes. "Can you tell what I'm thinking? I mean, can you read the details...?"

"Leucothean have no psychic abilities." The corners of her mouth were turned up. Whether the look was amused or enigmatic secrecy, Clare couldn't tell. "You have my word. I won't know anything you don't speak aloud. Close your eyes, please, and hold the time you were angry in your mind."

Clare did as she was told, and Thetis tenderly anointed her eyelids with the salve. She pictured their small apartment on Daeth, the exposed brick of the living room wall and the three half-circle windows that let in southern light during the afternoons. Clare remembered it in vivid detail. The music coming through the wall from their neighbor's apartment, the dishes in the sink, and the distorted reflection of Laikyn standing behind her and waiting for the eruption.

The smell of the man, the taste of him in her mouth when Clare came in from school early. Just remembering the moment of discovery made Clare furious, and she balled her hands into fists until her fingernails bit into the tender flesh of her palms. Thetis brushed her thumbs across Clare's cheeks, under her eyes.

"Good. Your face is flush. Your anger with her was intense. Did it last long?"

Months. They had almost separated, but Clare had eventually made her peace with it. She couldn't forget, but she couldn't withhold forgiveness from the only person she'd ever loved. Laikyn's apology was heartfelt. What she'd done was borne from curiosity rather than desire. The offer had been extended, and she had never been with anyone but Clare. She thought using her mouth and hands would make it easier, but she knew she was wrong. Clare's forgiveness only came when she realized how painful it was to Laikyn as well.

"Never do that again."

"Never. I never will, Rani Clare."

"There," Thetis whispered. "The only thing stronger than anger - true anger - is the forgiveness that comes afterward. The love that overtakes anger is the strongest in the world. Like the first rays of sunlight through storm clouds. Breathe deeply, Clare. The scent of the oils will be a comfort to you in times of need. To follow the trail and learn the truth of what happened to your sister, to your lover, you will need the strength of that post-fight love."

Clare realized that her cheeks and forehead were wet, and the smell of the oil was overwhelming. She felt lightheaded.

"You're not getting me high, are you?"

"High?"

"Intoxicated?"

"Oh. No. The effects you're feeling are temporary, but they create lasting peace." She touched the tip of Clare's chin with her thumb. Clare was surprised that despite the amount of oil on her face, none of it was dripping. She inhaled again and let the breath out slowly. "You should be calm, relaxed, and in control of your emotions for the next five days."

Clare opened her eyes. "Let's hope that will be enough."

Thetis put the bottle in Clare's hand and folded her fingers over it. "You may keep this. If you require another session, I will be happy to oblige."

"How long do I have to leave the oil on my face?"

"Until you bathe. When it dries, it will be unnoticeable."

Clare smiled. "Great. So I'm going to have this goop all over my face for the walk back to my quarters. Shouldn't cause too many comments."

Thetis shrugged. "You can always wait here until you are presentable. I have nothing better to do, so I shall wait with you." She gathered the excess material of her robes into her lap and crossed one leg over the other. "Tell me of Laikyn. Happier memories this time."

Clare shook her head and reached up to scratch her cheek, changing the angle at the last second to touch her hair instead. She wasn't sure if she wanted to share her private, personal memories of Laikyn with this near-stranger. But after the anguish of the past few months, combined with the shocking revelation that the *Juno* was connected to the first confirmed Harvestmen sighting in her adult life, maybe it was just what she needed.

"Laikyn is a lieutenant colonel in the Marine's linguistic unit..."

Thetis nodded for her to continue. Clare went on, and didn't stop talking until long after the oil on her face had dried and vanished from sight.

Captain Josiah Harp owed a message to his superiors, as well as one to Regent Nereus as to why Thetis wasn't being delivered to their temporary colony as scheduled. He assumed the note to the Leucothean priest would be the easier one to write, since he wasn't required to provide details, but he couldn't bring himself to begin either note. He tapped his finger against the edge of his desk and stared at the blank white screen until he pushed away from the desk in disgust. He stood to stretch his legs and ended up leaving his office to stalk the corridors of his ship in the hopes inspiration would find him better if he was on the move.

He was near the public dining area when he was found in a more literal sense by the head of the ship's Marine unit. Gunnery Sergeant Nasim Senech hurried to match his captain's speed, then paused and waited to be addressed before he spoke.

"Sir, word has gotten out concerning the current mission, not to mention the events aboard the *Prospekt*. People are aware there's a chance we'll run into the Harvestmen when we arrive at the *Juno*'s last known location. A few of the non-military officers were wondering if there was a possibility we might stop at a safe haven along the way and give them a chance to disembark."

Harp shook his head. "Sorry, Gunny. That won't be possible."

"Understood, sir. May I give them a reason?"

He stopped and looked back toward his office. "It's the same reason I can't bring myself to write those damned messages. We're putting off chartered business to go on this potential goose chase, and I owe our employers a reason why we're being delayed. The Command will have my ass if we run off without giving a heading or a reason for deviating from our course. God forbid anything happens and we get stuck out here where no one knows to look for us."

He took off his glasses and rubbed the bridge of his nose as he calmed himself down. He finally met Nasim's gaze again. "Despite all of that, I cannot in good conscience let people off his ship. People will talk, and I have absolutely no doubt the subject of that talk will be Harvestmen. We drop off even a half dozen people at the next viable world, they'll tell anyone who will listen. Then the story spreads, and we have a panic. I'd rather know for certain what we're facing before we frenzy the entire sector."

"Aye, sir. I'll let them know."

He started to turn away, but Harp stopped him. "Gunny. Tell them... tell them that if worse comes to worst, I'll do everything in my power to protect the people of this vessel."

"I don't have to tell anyone that, sir. I'll start spreading the word that no one is going anywhere."

"Try not to make it sound like a prison sentence, if you can."

He nodded and walked away, and Harp continued his falsely casual stroll. He remembered the first Harvestmen war, the ACRA Attritions that tried to contain them. The Peaceful Sea hadn't officially been involved in the fighting, but in reality no suitably-armed ship had avoided fighting. He was a Lieutenant Junior Grade at the time, stationed aboard the *Early*. They had been conscripted to assist an ACRA vessel in 'cleansing' a moon where the Harvestmen had been running amok.

Harp had been on the bridge when the order came. Only he and Commander Alec Rubin had been in a position to see the life signs detector before and after the weapons fired. Seventy-four heat signatures below ten Celsius - the Harvestmen - had been annihilated. The three-hundred and eighty heat signatures between thirty and forty degrees Celsius had also vanished. They had been given the order to evacuate, an order that ignored the fact some of these backwaters didn't have the ships on hand to facilitate their escape. The extraction order was a way for Command to shrug and say, "We told them to leave. It's not our fault they didn't listen."

The human cost was declared an acceptable risk to prevent the Harvestmen from spreading to other colonies. Killing nearly four hundred souls on a small colony on a nameless moon was preferable to Harvestmen reaching a large port town like Inlirs or Tromei. He knew exactly what ACRA would do if word got out Harvestmen had been spotted in this sector. They would send ships, a fleet of expendable humans ordered to stop the advance at all costs.

He made the decision and turned back to his office to make the report before he lost his nerve. He wasn't going to be the captain who set off another wave of genocide, and he wouldn't have the blood of so many soldiers and civilians on his hands. If the Harvestmen were back, he would do everything in his power to stop them now before they began to spread.

As he walked, he forcefully quieted the voice that wondered if the *Prospekt*'s captain had made the same vow.

XI. JUNO

The question soon became, well, if the Harvestmen don't have interplanetary means of transport, then how did they travel from one place to another? Shouldn't, yes, shouldn't it have been a simple matter to contain them? Hardly. Oh, hardly! For you see, as we poor humans fled their evil, we also gave them the means to proliferate. Harvestmen are far from the mindless beasts they appear to be. Their strategy of cleaning up their crimes to lure in more victims is evidence of that. Once they realized that humans would grab the nearest spaceship and run away to someplace safer, they adjusted their plans accordingly. Pregnant females would stow away aboard the lifeboats and remain hidden until they arrived wherever it was they were going. Then they would find a quiet spot to lay their eggs and, well, the cycle continued.

The discovery of this tactic led to the unfortunate decision to... ahem. Excuse me. We decided to stop colonists from evacuating from areas infested by the Harvestmen. Quarantines, and sure some could call them ghettos and rightly so, were set up. Eventually some said that if you saw a Harvestman, the most humane course of action would be to just shoot yourself in the head and save everyone else the trouble.

~ former ACRA Vice Admiral Eldred Clarke

The Crow's Nest was alight with the glow of every computer, as if the *Paralus* had sprouted eyes that were currently looking in every possible direction. Anais was in the middle of her second shift, kept alert by non-narcotic Second Wind inhalers Dr. Monroe prescribed to her. The rest of the command staff were gathered on the bridge. According to the coordinates they retrieved from the *Prospekt*'s records, they were nearing the *Juno*'s final resting place. No one wanted to be left out of the first sighting, despite the ship's time being a few hours before First Light.

They had been decreasing speed, and Anais shifted her gaze from monitor to monitor, awaiting the telltale signal that would announce they had reached their destination. She was about to accept the cruel fact she would have to hand off the controls to her relief to go get some rest when she spotted an object relatively near their position. She cranked her chair over to the monitor that was sounding a quiet alarm to get her attention and struggled to maintain her calm as she confirmed size and shape before she opened a line to Captain Harp.

"I see her, Captain. The *Juno* is two hundred thousand kilometers below us and six degrees to north-starboard. Changing bearing to intercept. We'll have visual confirmation in eighteen minutes."

Clare glanced over to Harp, who nodded at her. "Anais confirmed a sighting. She's bringing us to it now."

She nodded and braced her arms on the rail that circled the command area. Two years. She'd spent two years wondering what happened to Laikyn, and now they were on their way to find the answers. Actually, they were just confirming the answers they already had. She didn't want to believe the Harvestmen had been involved, but it was the most plausible answer. She was now mostly focused on not thinking about how Harvestmen killed, and how horrifying Laikyn's final moments must have been.

Captain Harp turned to Nasim. "Gunny, prepare a team to board the *Juno*."

Nasim looked at Clare, who had straightened to fix her eyes on the back of her Captain's head. "Pardon, sir, but shouldn't you be saying that to me?"

He turned to face her. "You lost someone extremely important to you on that ship, Commander. I can't risk~"

"Sir, I'm grateful, but your caution is unnecessary. Laikyn has been gone for two years. I've been preparing myself for this moment for half that time. I always expected to find out over a wave or in a news broadcast. But I have the chance to walk onto the ship she died on, see where she breathed her last... Sir, I'm not only capable, I have to do this."

Nasim said, "All things being equal, Captain, I would prefer to have her on my team when we go over there. The worst that can happen is that we'll run into Harvestmen, and she proved on the *Prospekt* that she's the kind of soldier you want between you and those monsters."

Clare nodded her thanks to him, and Harp relented. "Okay, Commander Cossin. You've proven yourself in worse situations. But if you have any doubts once you're over there, I want you to hand over command to Gunny Senech and hightail it back here. Understood?"

"Aye, sir. I'll start preparing a team immediately."

Lieutenants Tomas Green and Articulate Right had, unsurprisingly, already requested to be left off any boarding team that went over to the *Juno*. One run-in with the Harvestmen experience was plenty for a lifetime, and Clare didn't hold it against them. Lieutenant Hass, on the other hand, was eager for a second chance to face down the biggest threat the galaxy had ever faced. Clare was wary of his excitement, but she would rather have someone who was gung-ho than force someone who wasn't willing.

Tobias Odon, an engineer, and weapons officer Henderson Kite also accepted, and Nasim got a handful of his Marines to provide escort for every member of the team. On Captain Harp's order, Marines would also be stationed at the hatch, along the umbilical connecting the ships, and blocking both ends of the corridor leading to the airlock. He wasn't taking any chances.

Clare applied a touch of Thetis' oil behind her ears before she suited up. The scent soon filled her re-circulated air and she breathed in deeply. She checked her Fore-Arms to ensure they had a full charge and looked up to see Nasim was doing to same. She made sure the other Marines and their lieutenants were otherwise occupied before she stepped closer to tap the side of his boot with hers.

"Hey." He looked up. "Thanks for sticking up for me."

"No problem. I have longer legs than you. If we have to run, you'll distract the Harvestmen long enough for me to get away."

"Good luck outrunning anyone after I shoot out your knees."

Nasim whistled between his teeth. "You play dirty. All right, it comes to that, I'll throw one of the privates."

Clare chuckled. When it came to Harvestmen, running wasn't a sign of cowardice even to a Marine. The gallows humor was meant to lighten the tension. They had seen the *Juno* framed in the sensors, adrift and lifeless with no signs of damage to the outer hull. Clare couldn't help but think of which small porthole along the side looked out from Laikyn's room. The Captain had given them a go, and they were now waiting for the ships to be aligned so the umbilical could be extended and latched on.

The yellow light over the airlock switched to blue. Nasim took a deep breath and wagged his thick eyebrows at Clare before settling his helmet over his head. Clare did the same and, a moment later, their holographic heads flickered into view. They stepped forward and opened the hatch together, and Clare peered out onto the umbilical.

She remembered the sound of the Harvestman, the way it had lunged at her before she destroyed it with a single well-placed blast. She was grateful the helmets didn't allow smell to transmit; medics who had been on battlefields reported that a live Harvestman's skin reeked in a way that it took human corpses three days to achieve.

Harp spoke to them over their comms. "We're hooked up and matching velocity. Someone didn't shut down the *Juno*'s engines before dying. Anais has scanned the ship thrice and reports no, repeat no, thermal reports above zero Celsius. Even if they were hibernating, the Harvestmen would be hotter than that. Proceed with caution, nonetheless."

"Aye, sir."

She and Nasim stepped back to allow two of his Marines to go first. They opened the hatch to the other ship and moved with choreographed grace into the abandoned corridor. Nasim stepped closer to Clare. His projected face flickered, turned blue-gray by the imagers, and she could see the faint ring of his helmet underneath the hologram.

"Are you sure you're up for this? Just between you and me. I'll back you all the way no matter what, but I wanted to make absolutely certain before we cross this umbilical and–"

"I'm fine, Nasim. But thank you."

He nodded and looked toward the open hatch. It hung wide, beckoning to them like the mouth of a cave. She remembered Laikyn telling her fairy stories of knights and damsels in distress. The story of Orpheus and Eurydice. Fire-breathing dragons, trolls, gnomes, highwaymen, bears, demons, blood-drinking bats.

Nothing good came out of caves. And no good came from going into them.

One of the Marines called back and Nasim tilted his head to the side to listen. "Understood." He looked at Clare and relayed, "Main corridors are clear, no signs of life. No signs of death, either. Harvestmen have done their typical bang-up job of washing up. You know, we ought to domesticate the damn things. Hire them to scrub a house once every month or so."

Clare led the way toward the hatch. Her right arm was extended, the Fore-Arm lit and ready for discharge. She had her left hand on top of the mechanism to manually fire multiple loads if necessary. "The only downside to that is they'd eat your neighbors."

"Fuck the neighbors. I'm more worried they'll try to unionize. Then where will we be? Try negotiating with a blue-collar carnivore..."

Their good humor evaporated as they moved closer to the dead ship. Nasim paused at the airlock and allowed Clare to go first. It wasn't just deference to her rank, but an acknowledgement that this was more than just a mission to her. She nodded her thanks to him and stepped through. The life support and gravity was off, so the ground sucked at her magnetized boot and sealed it down with a solid thunk.

The Marines who had gone ahead left light sticks that hung in the air where they had been released. The green trail hovered and spun at waist-height through the corridor, casting a strange underwater glow over the curved walls. Clare stepped forward and Nasim joined her.

"You want to take the bridge again?" he asked.

Clare nodded and turned. "Lieutenants Kite and Odon, check their armory. Lieutenant Hass, stay here and guard the way home. You see anything that's not us, blow its head off."

"Aye, ma'am."

She motioned for Nasim to follow her, and she led him into the ship where her lover died.

XII. GRAVEYARD

"You'll never catch me using those Profiles, and no one on my crew wears 'em, neither!"

"You prefer seeing the helmet? Looking back an' not knowin' which member of your crew is standing behind you?"

"That's what we have ID badges for, kest it! I won't have it."

The other soldiers laughed at the old captain's fire and then looked at each other. Oh, superstitious fool!, the looks said. The subject of their delight stared each of them down with a scowl and a twisted lip and silenced them with a hand dropped flat on the table. The laughter faded and the men turned to face him with the proper respect. He let the silence hang before he spoke again.

"Sure, they're fine at a distance. Them cameras do a fine job makin' a man's face. Stand even two feet 'way from a man with the Profile runnin' and you'd be hard-pressed to say whether he had a helmet on a'tall. But when you get closer, you can see the color ain't right. And the eyes. Damn holo-cams never get the eyes right. They're flat. Lifeless. You get right up on a Profile and you ain't never gonna mistake it for a real person. Cause with that pale skin and eyes that are just flat plain wrong... you might's well be lookin' at a corpse."

~ excerpt from *Missed Horizon*, Book 2 of the epic Age of Thrust series

The yellow running lights that signaled a mission was underway lit Engineering in sickly amber. Sadiq Malki was accustomed to the light, so he didn't allow it to affect his concentration. He had to adjust the ship's speed and velocity to accommodate the *Juno*, and now he was nudging the engines to avoid overtaxing them. They had been designed for one ship, and doubling the mass they had to stop required a bit of ballet. Radka Saric was his second pair of eyes, a fail-safe measure he was grateful for in this particular instance. Every few seconds he thought about Declan, over on another ship likely infested with those horrific Harvestmen. Foolhardy man. The night before he'd declared his intent to volunteer for the away team, insisting he had to face his fear or risk being consumed by it.

And what of my fear? Sadiq wondered. Even with the Marines there, lieutenants were always the front line. Command staff protected each other, and the support crew was there to make sure their officers got back in one piece. Lieutenants and Marines were expendable. Hell, he doubted Commander Cossin and Gunny Senech even knew Declan's first name.

"You're in the red, 'Diq."

He blinked at his readout and cursed as he made a minute adjustment. The readings leveled off and the whirr behind him slowed, then ceased.

"Thanks, Radka."

"It's what I'm here for." She paused. "I would be in the same boat, if it was James over there."

Sadiq nodded brusquely. "Right. No sense dwelling on it. Let's just make sure they have a smooth journey."

"Aye, sir."

He scratched his upper lip and put thoughts of his husband out of his mind. The *Paralus* and *Juno* were now connected by an umbilical, moving cautiously through space as one.

Anais was calm. Through her screens and on the monitors, the *Juno* seemed to take up the entirety of space. It loomed before her like a tarp had been drawn over their ship, but she could still see a sliver of stars to the port side. She was determined not to faint or panic or make a spectacle out of herself again. She checked behind her to make sure she was alone in the Crow's Nest and removed the small phial from the inside pocket of her uniform vest. Thetis had told her to use it to stem any encroaching panic. While she felt fine, she knew it could boil over in an instant. Better to take advantage of it now, while things were quiet.

She cracked the top and smelled it, then pressed the lip against her cupped palm and turned it over.

She used her small finger to draw symbols in the oil. The Holy Staff, the Leaf, and Infinity. She made a fist and closed her eyes. "Rani Clare Cossin. Rani Clare Cossin. To safety, to light, out of the hostile darkness, to light. To safety. Rani Clare Cossin." She kissed her knuckles and opened her eyes. Her navigation now had to account for the dead weight they were dragging underneath them, making sure it didn't smash into anything while their people were aboard.

As she worked, she continued murmuring the old familiar prayer under her breath.

Kira Gray feared the Harvestmen in a way most species didn't. The Op'tra heard the Harvestmen before any members of their species knew what they looked like. The clicking-clack of their clawed feet and hands, the way they skittered across walls and ceilings, the sharp snaps as they dropped from a perch and landed on the ground... Harvestmen emitted a high-pitched shriek before they attacked. Humans never reported it because it was inaudible to them, but Op'tra originally called the beasts Shriekers because of that sound.

Op'tra knew what a feasting Harvestman sounded like. As she waited for contact from the away team, she imagined she could hear that sound echoing down the corridors of the *Paralus*. She was tense, hadn't even bothered to flirt with Clare before departure. She rested her hand on the console and listened through their communicators. The silence crowded around her, broken only by the solid thumping of the team's magnetized boots as they moved through the ship. They occasionally spoke quietly to one another, but for the most part they respected the lost crew by staying quiet.

Kira extended her senses to "see" the room around her. No one was paying attention to her, too wrapped up in their own fears to share someone else's, and she reached up to increase the volume on her headset. Each whisper suddenly became a near-shout. Any loud noises would be painful, but if it meant she could hear danger coming even one second sooner, she was willing to risk temporary deafness.

As the captain's files downloaded from the command chair, Clare scanned the bridge for signs of damage. The Harvestmen had done their usual crackerjack job of covering up. Their Marine escorts were checking out the other rooms on the command level, and they had orders to return to the umbilical immediately after making their rounds. The Captain didn't want anyone onboard longer than absolutely necessary.

Nasim returned from the captain's office and reported no sign of anything. Clare pressed her lips together and looked at the back of the bridge. A linguistics station was positioned in a small alcove near the bridge's entrance, and for a moment she had a vision of Laikyn seated there with a small headset on. Her eyes closed, a line of concentration between her brow, her lips moving carefully as she translated the captain's message to another vessel.

"You okay?" Nasim asked.

She looked over at him and then down at the computer. "No. Hold on." She bent down and turned on the monitor. There was still power in the ship, and it activated immediately. She opened the menu and scanned for the Personnel files. Nasim crossed the bridge and stood behind her, frowning as she scrolled through the names.

"What are you doing?"

"I have to see where she lived."

Nasim started to say something, but the vowel died in his throat. He looked toward the access hatch. When he finally spoke, his voice was lowered to a hushed whisper. "We don't have time for this, Clare. Honestly, I wish we did..."

She turned to face him. "We're going to have to scuttle this ship the way we did the *Prospekt*. I'm not going to cope well with that if I don't at least... symbolically say goodbye to her."

"Then do it here! She was stationed right here. The Captain said no one~"

"I know what Captain Harp said. I have to do this, Nasim. Head back to the umbilical if you want, but I'm doing this."

He sighed. "Clare..."

She checked the file again and memorized the number of Laikyn's room. She turned and walked past Nasim. A few seconds later, she heard him curse in the headset and his heavy footsteps followed her to the ladder.

"Thanks."

"Buy me dinner," Nasim snapped.

They descended together, and Clare led the way through the

creepily-abandoned Home level. She used her light to read the numbers beside each door until she found the right one. She pressed her gloved hand to the panel beside the door, but it didn't read her thick gloved fingers as human. She sighed and looked at the seam where the two halves of the door met. "We'll have to force it."

"Dinner and dessert," Nasim groused as he stepped forward. "Moving goddamn doors... Captain will have your hide for this."

"I don't care." Together they managed to get the door open wide enough for her, and Nasim stepped into the gap to keep it from closing while Clare was inside. He braced his foot against one door, his back against the other, and kept a look out for any unwelcome guests. Clare stepped past him and turned her light to maximum illumination. It cast the room into sharp relief, with a white light that was almost a physical presence. She stood just inside the door and drank it in, eyes welling up as she looked at the last place Laikyn had called home.

It was a standard PSV officer's quarters. The bedroom was to the right, through a door that slid closed manually, and a kitchen area was to the left. In between was the living area, with a narrow tinted window that provided a poor to middling view, depending on whether any planets were in visual range. Clare recognized the back wall from countless videos and she moved to the ugly red couch where Laikyn had been sitting when she made the calls.

Lieutenant Hass spoke over the comms. "Commander Cossin, Gunny Senech, do you read us?"

"Five by five," Nasim said. "We're fine. We're just taking a little detour."

Hass was silent for a moment. "Sightseeing, sir?"

Nasim laughed. "Something like that. We'll see you in ten."

Clare noted the deadline and moved toward the bedroom door. A small twin bed was tucked against the wall with maroon blankets tucked up underneath the two pillows. She was about to turn away when she noticed the picture over the bed wasn't the typical artwork typically associated with crew quarters. She stepped closer and held her light at an angle so it didn't obscure what was behind the glass frame.

It was a relatively simple crayon drawing of a place Clare recognized immediately. It was a white cliff that looked over a ravine on Merrik, with twin rock towers rising in the distance. She and Laikyn had parked there on one of their shore leaves after being told that the sun set perfectly between the two towers at that location. They had packed a picnic and, once the light was gone, wrapped themselves in the blanket and made love as the stars came out.

In the white space at the top of the drawing the artist had written "To Auntie Laken. From Lorelei."

Clare frowned and stepped closer. She and Laikyn had no family but each other.

"Clare, we gotta hustle."

"I know." She reached up and lifted the picture off the wall. As she did, the name Lorelei clicked in her brain and she remembered the text of Laikyn's final message to her. The final message anyone had received from the *Juno*.

"Mission progressing well. Nebulas (nebulae?) shining in the distance, so beautiful. Sirens on the shoreline and wax in my ears, love."

Lorelei, the siren who sang ships to their doom. "Why?" she whispered.

"We gotta go," Nasim insisted, calling to her from the other room rather than over the radio.

She sighed and tucked the picture under her arm. She would decipher its meaning later when they were safely back aboard the *Paralus*. She returned to the main room. "I think I found something."

"Great!" Nasim said with manufactured glee. "Let's get out of here before they leave us behind." He opened a channel. "We're on our way back, Hass."

The Harvestman loomed suddenly in the corridor, framed by the twisted shape of Nasim's body. Clare lifted her Fore-Arm to fire, but it moved too quickly for her to get a shot off. Nasim turned as the creature's bladed arm sliced through his leg and severed it just below the knee. He fell forward and the doors started to close as the Harvestman dug its blade into Nasim's chest. Clare lunged forward and grabbed the front of Nasim's suit, pulling him in as the Harvestman's claw ripped his chest open.

Nasim's blood began to fill the air around them, columns of it reforming into globes as it spun in a merry dance. She let go of him and he dangled in the air just inside the door. He was already dead, but she wasn't going to allow his corpse to be eaten by a fucking monster. The door snapped shut on the Harvestman's maw spread wide in a howl that didn't reach her ears in the vacuum of space.

The attack had lasted less than ten seconds. Clare knelt down to confirm Nasim was dead, but the holo-Profile of his face left little doubt. She moved to touch his cheek, but her hand came up short against the physical barrier of his opaque helmet. She shut off the Profile and Nasim's death mask vanished.

Clare stood and faced the door, alone in her late lover's dark quarters with Harvestmen about to beat down the door.

XIII. BLOODLETTING

"Blood and bone and muscle and stone
The Harvestman eats you when you're alone
Skin and teeth and hair and eyeball
The Harvestman eats you, eats you all."
~ graffiti

The away team heard Nasim's screams. The horrific sounds transmitted across the aether to the *Paralus* communications array, where Kira heard it all in sickening detail. Clare heard the sound of Hass and the Marines deploying on Harp's orders as she stood with her Fore-Arm raised in a pathetic show of defense against the closed door. She tensed, eyes wide and sweating under her helmet as she listened to the off-putting silence from the other side of the door. Nasim's body floated like a piece of untethered furniture next to the door, still spilling blood that filled the air like grisly banners.

Clare quietly relayed her position to the team, and Hass confirmed they were on their way. In the same half-voice, she explained the situation to Captain Harp and everyone back on the *Paralus*. Captain Harp didn't bother to assure her that they would get her out in one piece; they both knew the procedure too well for the lie to work even as cold comfort. She looked around the room for ways to get an advantage, but there was nothing that would outweigh the fact she was penned in like cattle.

The door trembled with the silent impact of the Harvestman slamming into it from the other side. She heard nothing, no sound whatsoever issuing from the creature that was, without a doubt furious, and that only made it more frightening. It had approached without a single warning, no tell-tale sounds to alert them to its presence. Sometimes she fucking hated space.

She flexed her fingers against the trigger of her Fore-Arm. Everything in her wanted to fire a warning shot, but she was going to save up the charge for when it would actually do some good. Another thud, and she realized with dread that she wasn't sure how many Harvestmen were actually outside. What if the one that grabbed Nasim was just the first to arrive? What if one was trying to get in while the others finished off their prey?

"Lieutenant Hass... Do you have an ETA?" Silence. How many Harvestmen were aboard the ship? "Lieutenant Hass, do you read me? Anais? Kira?" The only sound was the beast slamming against the door of Laikyn's quarters. Clare backed away from the door and shut off the light so the room was thrown into total darkness.

"Where the *kest* did that thing come from?" Harp demanded.

Anais was deathly pale. "Sir, I don't know. I'm still not reading any life signs other than our people. They... were masked somehow." She swallowed the nausea that threatened to overtake her as she scanned the monitors that had betrayed her. Her hands shook on the controls as if they were full of energy and just waiting for her to tell them what to do. She looked at the schematics of the *Juno*, the display that should have told her Clare and Nasim were in danger, and she realized she knew where one of the fucking things was. She leaned forward and touched that screen's menu and began randomly playing with the controls.

The screen changed colors rapidly, swirling rainbows of heat signatures and ghost images, and then she saw it. "Oh, you're a *cold* bastard, aren't you?" she whispered. She opened her comm. Once she knew what to look for, she opened her coverage to the rest of the ship. Dozens of Harvestmen swarmed every deck. Most of them seemed confined to rooms for some reason, while others stalked the corridors. The away team members were too warm to register on this filter, so the ship seemed like a killing field without any prey.

But the Harvestmen knew the food was there. She could see it in the way they moved.

"Captain Harp, I have a visual on the Harvestmen. They're thirty degrees cooler than we've ever seen them. I have no idea why~"

"I don't care why, Navigator. Can you direct our team back to the umbilical? They're currently on Level 8 between the airlocks and the Home level."

Anais adjusted the filter again so she could see the human signatures as well as the Harvestmen and resisted the urge to curse. "Sir, the Harvestmen are surrounding them. Oh, God." She held her hands over the controls, helpless. She rubbed her fingers against her palm and breathed deeply, remembering Thetis' treatments. She looked again for an alternative and almost immediately spotted one.

"The shuttles. Sir, the away team can get to the shuttles from where they are. If they can get enough power to separate from the ship, we should be able to scoop them up."

"What about Commander Cossin?"

Dark blobs of cold bodies swarmed the area in front of the room where Clare was trapped. The color was so thick that she couldn't see the human signature through it. She swallowed again and choked out a response. "She's trapped, sir. Entirely cut off. She... won't make it, sir."

After a moment, he called Lieutenant Hass on the same frequency. The rescue mission was aborted and his team was ordered double-time to the shuttles.

Anais' eyes were wet with tears. "Clare? Can you read me? I'm sorry." She bit her lip and looked out the window.

"Prepare to disconnect the umbilical on my mark."

"Aye, sir," Anais whispered. Over the headset, she heard the sounds of battle. The away team had run into Harvestmen on their way to the shuttle. Only two, so they were rapidly dealt with. Since Henderson Kite was aboard the *Juno*, the weapons officer was Ahmad Jasem was given the hold order. Once they had confirmation the away team was clear, the ship would be immediately scuttled.

Anais closed her eyes and drew the signs of the Staff, the Leaf, and Infinity in the air in front of her. "Peace, Rani Clare Cossin. To peace. To silence. To peace. Rani Clare Cossin." Her voice broke on the last repetition of her friend's name, and she opened her eyes. She would have to pull the ship away fast so they wouldn't be caught in the *Juno*'s destruction.

She was given the order to disconnect the umbilical and start withdrawal.

Sadiq pressed his forehead against Radka's, his hands tight on her shoulders as she spoke to him softly in their native language. His eyes were closed, his dark eyelashes trembling as he struggled to remain calm. From what they overheard, Declan was safe and guiding his team to one of the shuttles to make a desperate escape from a ship overrun with Harvestmen. His fingers tensed but, although he was surely bruising his second in command, she made no complaint.

"The shuttle is away, sir," Anais reported.

"Understood. Lieutenant Jasem, once we're at a safe distance, I want you to kill every last one of the beasts on board that ship."

And Clare. You're killing Clare, too, sir.

She sent the "all-clear" to Jasem's console and looked out the screen for a physical view of the ship before it was destroyed. Its shuttle arced across the void between them and she was glad that the majority of their people would get out in one piece. The shuttle altered course due to some communication she hadn't picked up, and then two missiles streaked from the underside of the *Paralus*.

One hit the upper hull, and one disappeared below. The ship seemed to crunch in on itself, and its surface flared bright for one blinding moment, and then nothing.

Anais turned away from the screen, slipped from her chair, and slid along the wall until she could wrap her arms around her knees. They'd had two encounters with the Harvestmen, and they had suffered two casualties. Only two casualties. It was actually an amazingly good ratio. Maybe a record.

She pressed her face into the crook of her elbow and began to cry.

Twelve minutes earlier

Clare didn't know a single person who thought putting windows in a spaceship was a good idea. In order to be safe, they were made so incredibly thick that the views through them were mediocre at best. One designed suggested protecting both sides of the glass with force fields, but the power output was ridiculous. What was there to see in space? Just more space. Stars and nebulae and planets spinning. But convention dictated that crew quarters have windows, lest the crew suffer from claustrophobia in an enclosed shell of a room.

She used both of her Fore-Arms to destroy the window in Laikyn's quarters. The ship was completely without atmosphere, so she didn't have to worry about a breach. She worked furiously, using her entire charge on melting the fixtures. When the weapons sputtered and froze, she pulled off Nasim's Fore-Arms - with a muttered apology for her roughness - and finished the job. The glass broke, and she used furniture from the room to push it out of the way with extreme care.

Clare retrieved the maroon blanket off Laikyn's bed and awkwardly wrapped Nasim's body with it. She wasn't going to leave him behind if she could help it. She pinned the framed picture she had taken off Laikyn's wall under his arms and then secured the blanket so he wouldn't roll free.

She lifted him, initially surprised with how easy it was before she remembered that nothing had weight without gravity, and she hauled him over to the narrow hole in the side of the ship. She pushed him out first, gripping his shroud with one hand so he wouldn't float away as she edged out after him.

The Harvestmen continued to slam against the door; she could feel the vibrations in the deck now. There had to be more than one now. With her choices firmly outlined between drifting in the void with her friend's corpse and facing down a herd of hungry Harvestmen, she moved with more haste through the gap. She pulled Nasim to her, hugging him against her chest as she turned and braced her feet against the hull. She pushed off and extended to her full height, then dropped back down.

"You moron," she murmured. She managed to reach her suit controls and rested her fingers on the controls for her boot magnetics. She bent her knees, coiled like a spring, and pushed off. This time she shut off the magnets and she propelled herself outward away from the ship. She tried her radio again. "Anais? Captain Harp? Lieutenant Hass? Any-fucking-body?"

She lifted her head and saw, inverted and twisted above her so that it seemed to be happening upside down, a shuttle launch from the *Juno*. The umbilical was retracted, and the *Paralus* was moving back to a safe distance. Clare's eyes widened as she put the pieces together and realized what Captain Harp's plan was. He was willing to sacrifice her to save the rest of the away team, and to stop the Harvestmen from getting aboard the *Paralus*.

"It's a good plan," she whispered.

She saw the flash from the *Paralus*' weapons ports. She twisted and tried to push herself farther away from the ship as the missiles streaked past her to impact the vessel.

A heartbeat later and the *Juno* was gone. She looked up at her ship, looming massively above her but an impossibly far distance away.

"Commander Cossin to the *Paralus*. Come in, please. Anais, this is Clare. Kira? Anyone at all?"

No response was forthcoming. The shuttle of escapees changed its heading toward the ship's hangar. Once it was safe, Captain Harp would give the order and they'd get the hell away from this graveyard.

Adrift with a corpse and a busted radio, Clare breathed deep and smelled the oil Thetis had given her. She remembered her prayer that she would get off the ship safely and laughed. It was a macabre sound that echoed in her helmet as she and Nasim drifted. The prayer had been heard, and granted. For once, she'd gotten exactly what she'd asked for.

She wished she'd been more specific.

CHAPTER FOUR

XIV. WHISPERS

Warning! Your MCPS (Mechanical Counter-Pressure Suit) tanks contain NO MORE than four hours of air. This does not mean you have four hours of air.
~ standard signage in MCPS gear room

Translation: if you're ever still outside at the three hour mark, start kissing your ass goodbye.
~ graffiti in same

The *Juno's* shuttle docked safely, and a visibly shaken away team emerged from the rear hatch. The shuttle still had life support, so their helmets had been removed to reveal ashen, sweaty faces of the men and women who had gone aboard the doomed ship. Captain Harp was waiting when Lieutenant Hass emerged. He straightened his posture when he saw his captain. "Sir. I can't explain what happened over there. I don't even know what they were doing in the Home level."

"I think I have an idea. It wasn't your fault, Lieutenant. How are your men coping?"

"My~" He realized that with Nasim dead, he was the ranking Marine officer. He swallowed and looked down for a moment before he responded. "Shaken, sir. It was grim there for a moment until Anais found a way to the shuttles for us."

"We'll cover it all in the briefing. Are you up for it now, or should we postpone?"

"I think we'd all rather get it out of the way as soon as possible, Captain. The faster we can get these images out of our heads~"

"Understood. Get out of your gear and have everyone gather in the briefing room."

"Aye, sir."

The locker area was tomb-silent, and the team changed into their uniforms without comment. One or two took advantage of a quick shower to wash away the dry sweat from their encounter, but Hass went directly to the bridge. He saw Kira in her station and made his way over to her. She turned her head slightly in response to his approach, but kept her attention on her console. Her voice was soft, guarded. "Lieutenant."

"Ma'am. I wanted to make sure you were okay. I know you were listening~"

"It's all right, Lieutenant Hass." She smiled slightly. "But thank you for your concern. I'm glad you returned with... most of your team."

He nodded. "Right. My team." He looked and saw Captain Harp was watching them. He swallowed hard. "I should get into the briefing room and put my thoughts in order."

Kira dipped her chin, then turned back to him. "Oh, Lieutenant. Could you please ask your team to disconnect their radios?"

He frowned. "We turned off our radios on the shuttle. No reason to leave them on. Besides, they're all out of their EVA gear."

She turned to face him fully. "One channel is still active."

Harp joined them. "What's the problem, Ms. Gray?"

"Sir. I'm hearing white noise from an active comm link."

Hass said, "My team all disconnected theirs, sir."

"Are you sure of it?"

"Well. No, sir, but I'd be willing to stake a lot on it. The suits are all powered down as soon as we take them off. Everything gets turned off. So unless someone is still in their suit~" He glanced toward the viewscreen. "I mean. Two members of the team are theoretically still in their suits, but~"

"They would have been destroyed in the explosion," Kira said.

"I'm hearing a definite..." She lifted her chin slightly. "It's too quiet on the other end of the connection, sir. If I was hearing a radio that was on our ship, I'd hear background noises. Voices, engines, footsteps, but I don't hear anything."

Harp looked at Hass. "Could one of them have made it out?"

"I... don't know, sir. Commander Cossin was trapped in a private room when her radio went dead."

Harp touched his headset to open a channel. "Anais Quimby."

A few seconds later she responded, sniffling and making an effort to control her voice. Her call was filtered through the speaker so everyone on the bridge could hear her, and Harp regretted making that decision. She should have been allowed to cry in private. "Quimby here, Captain."

"I want you to scan the vicinity around the *Juno*'s last location for life signs. Anything at all. Open the scan to include active radio signals."

Kira turned back to her station. "Commander Cossin, do you read? Commander Cossin, this is the *Paralus*. Come on, you stubborn beauty, answer me."

"Oh my Goddess!" Anais shouted. "There's someone out there?"

"Human?" Hass said.

"Yes! It's... they're holding onto something. But there's a body out there. Body temperature is consistent with a human in an EVA suit."

Hass said, "Sir, if it's Commander Cossin~"

"Then why isn't she responding?" Harp interrupted. "She may have just gotten blown out of the wreckage."

Hass considered for a moment. "It's not her radio that's active. Her radio went dead when we were still on board. Anais said she's holding onto something, right? What if she recovered Gunny Senech's body and it's his radio that Kira is picking up? She can't answer if she can't hear."

Harp rubbed his thumb and forefinger over his mustache as he looked at the viewscreen. Even at the highest magnification, he doubted they would be able to see something as small as a human body. Everything in his head was telling him it was just a pair of tangled corpses. But even if that was true, his people deserved a respectful burial.

"Lieutenant Hass, I don't want to order you~"

"I'll have the shuttle prepped immediately, sir." He was already jogging off the bridge.

Harp turned to Kira. "Keep talking, Ms. Gray. There's a chance her radio is just glitching and she'll be able to hear some of what you're saying."

"Aye, sir."

He walked to stand next to his command chair and looked out into the void. There was so much emptiness between them and the spot where the *Juno* had been laid to rest. It was akin to trying to find a single lifeboat in the Mediterranean Sea. Hass could lock onto the radio signal and narrow down the search, but that would only give him the general vicinity of the bodies.

There were more important concerns at the moment, like the fact Commander Cossin had been using air for an hour before the *Juno* was destroyed, and it had been another ninety minutes since her radio fell silent. She had, at best, another hour and a half before her oxygen tanks bottomed out and she asphyxiated.

"You're not very good company, Nasim. Not a very good dancer, either." She gasped as she took her next breath and rolled her eyes. "Shut up, Clare. You're using air." She giggled at the accidental rhyme and closed her eyes. "Clare's air. No air for Clare. Beware the lack of air up there. Out there." She smiled and tightened her grip on Nasim's body. "Light on your feet, Gunny. I didn't expect that. Must be all that time wearing your wife's skin."

The *Paralus* still hung above her. She wondered why they were hanging around. It had, after all, been three weeks since she left the *Juno*.

Hold on, no. That couldn't be right. Her air would have run out long before three weeks. Of course her air *was* running out. So who could say how long she'd been adrift.

She gasped again, a wheezing sound that made her throat feel tight.

"I think I'm going to take off my helmet. How many people's," another wheeze, "obituaries get to say 'Head Exploded'?"

Static filled her ears and Clare cried out in surprise. "~bitch~"

"I thought I just heard Kira's voice," Clare said. "You would have liked Kira, Laikyn. She flirts with me, but it's all right. She's asexual." She tilted her head. Wait. The body she was holding wasn't Laikyn's. Whose was it? Why was she holding a dead body?! She nearly let go of it before she remembered it was important. She could remember the why later. She hugged it tight and said, "I'm sorry I almost let you go, whoever you are."

Nasim.

Right.

Nasim was dead and wrapped in Laikyn's bedding. Clare remembered the affair, when she caught Laikyn with a cock in her mouth, and she'd sworn the next man she found in Laikyn's bed would end up dead. Look at that! She was psychic!

She snorted, then wheezed. Her hands felt the shape of Nasim's air pack. "Hog. Hoarding all this~gasp~air when you're dead. Incon~wheeze~siderate jerk."

"~you better answer me. Please, Clare."

"I'm *trying* to have a *conversation!*" she shouted.

"Commander?"

The relief evident in Kira's voice made Clare smile. It made her feel safe and loved. "I was just telling Laikyn you're asexual, so it's okay, even though we flirt, you'll never fuck me."

"Commander, we're looking for you. Okay? Lieutenant Hass is in a shuttle, and he's about to launch~"

"Say hi to Kira, baby."

"~Commander! I need you to listen to me."

"She's an Op'tra. Really good ears. Pretty, too."

Kira barked, "Listen to me, you stubborn bitch. You listen, or I'll never speak to you again, do you hear me?"

"She's so bossy," Clare growled. "Yes! I hear you." She wheezed and, for a horrible moment, she thought she wouldn't be able to draw in any more air. The panic had a grounding effect on her. She blinked. "Kira...?"

"I'm here, gorgeous. God, it's good to hear your voice."

"I'm outside the ship, Kira."

"I know. You're running out of air, but Lieutenant Hass is on his way in a shuttle. He's going to pick you up, but he's going to need help. Is there any way you can... you can announce yourself?"

Clare took as deep a breath as she dared and began to shout. Kira yelped in pain.

"No, that~ Clare. You're not thinking clearly, darling. Lieutenant Hass is in a shuttle. Do you see him?"

Clare resented being asked to look around. Didn't Kira have sensors on the ship? She lifted her head and scanned the space. "Our ship is *big*, Kira."

"You're looking for a little ship, Clare."

"There is it, it is there." She twisted and she and Nasim's body began spiraling. "Whoops. Round and round."

"Clare, you need to make him see you. You're out in the middle of space, and he has no idea where to go to pick you up. Understand? He's going to need your help."

It sounded like a lot of work. She was starting to relax. Her eight months of drifting like this had really taught her patience.

Eight months... no. Wait. Yeah. She looked at her arm and saw Nasim's Fore-Arm strapped there. "Oh! Tell him to look for the lights, Kira." She wrapped her fingers around the trigger and began firing. The force of the shots propelled their spin, but she kept shooting. Beams of yellow-green light spread through space and dissipated after a few dozen yards, but she kept it up. They were spinning faster, and now she completed a revolution in time to see the shots dissipating in the air.

"It's so pretty! Can you see it, Kira?"

"...no, Clare, I can't. But Lieutenant Hass does. He's on his way."

"All right."

"You can stop firing now, Commander."

"Right."

Spinning. Drifting. She wondered if she could get dizzy in space. Was dizziness a result of gravity on the brain or blood or... and she really only had one point of visual reference. Well, two if she counted the man in the EVA suit. But he was new, so he didn't count. She spun around and around. She thought about her obituary. Head exploding would be awesome, but "spun into the sun" was epic. And it rhymed!

"It rhymes, Lieutenant Hass!"

"I'm sure it does, Commander."

He made her stop spinning, and Clare closed her eyes again. She'd been asleep when he grabbed her, she was pretty sure, and she wanted to go back to sleep again. It was comforting to sleep. She dozed off and, when she woke, Dr. Monroe was kissing her and pinching her nose. Her face was hot and cold at the same time. Her skin felt boiling, but the room was cold. She was out of her mask. She was drenched in sweat. She was sore all over, in the joints and in her bones, and she gasped when Kali stopped kissing her.

"Commander? Sir!"

Captain Harp knelt next to her, and Kali brushed the hair back off Clare's sweaty forehead. He smiled and put his hand on her shoulder.

"Welcome back, Commander."

She nodded, frowned as she tried to remember where she had

gone, then let her head fall back to the deck with a solid thud. Her last conscious thought was that "Survived two Harvestmen attacks, emergency spacewalk and asphyxiation; immediately died from concussion in hangar" would be the most ridiculous obituary ever.

XV. Recovery

"Sure, it's a nice concept. It sounds good in movies, right? 'No one gets left behind.' But how many people are you willing to lose to get back one soldier. That soldier made a choice, just like you did. A good soldier would rather sacrifice themselves than have you risk your ass coming back for them. Don't get killed following some koan. Honor your fellow soldier's sacrifice by getting yourself home in one piece. Honor them by keeping their memories alive."
~ standard Marine training lecture

The first surprise was that she woke up. Even the throbbing headache was welcome as evidence she had survived. Monitors were attached to the backs of both forearms, and she lifted one to see what she could deduce from the information on it. Five blue circles, two green lines, and a circle with a red dot spinning around its perimeter. Clare figured out that it either meant she was going to live or that she was very near death. Either way, she was conscious, so she put her arms back down and looked at the woman seated next to her bed.

In her hazy moments immediately after waking, she saw the dark hair and pink skin and thought it was Laikyn. But now she could see it was Anais. She had pulled her feet up into the chair, her knees splayed to either side with her hands dangling in the butterfly shape her legs made. Her head lolled to one side, and her mouth was slightly open with the limpness of sleep. Clare watched her until she fell asleep again and, when she woke, Anais was awake, too.

"Hey, sleepy," she said.

Anais had dropped her feet to the floor, and she leaned forward to touch Clare's hand. "Hey, Commander. You've been out for a long time. Nearly two days."

"You watchin' over me?"

Tears filled Anais' eyes. "If I am, I'm not doing a very good job of it."

Clare frowned.

"Two Harvestmen attacks, Commander. You went onto two ships I told you were empty, and you got cornered by the bastards *twice*. You should have known they were there. If I'd done my job, you'd have known they were there." She sniffled and ran her wrist under her nose. "I'm going to resign."

"What? Don't..."

"The first time we got lucky. Second time..." She looked down and Clare pushed herself up against the pillows.

"Hey. Look at me. I don't know what's happening with these fucking things, but they're not the same Harvestmen ACRA wiped out twenty years ago. They're not following the rulebook we wrote on how to deal with them. They're colder, they're craftier. If you had seen them this last time, I wouldn't speak to you because I'd think you were a mole for their side. Even if you are prettier than any Harvestman I've ever seen."

That got a laugh, and Anais wiped her cheeks with the back of her hand.

"Don't blame yourself for what happened. Nasim's death was my..." She wet her lips. "It was my fault he died. If we'd just gone back to the umbilical after downloading the info we were there for, the Harvestmen wouldn't have snuck up on us and the other team wouldn't have gotten cut off from the umbilical. Them finding a clear path to the shuttle... that was you, wasn't it?"

Anais shook her head. "Anyone could've..."

"But you did. Anais, don't quit because I screwed up. Don't blame yourself for my stupid choices. I put everyone at risk and you saved them. Thank you."

Anais took a deep breath. "Yeah. Well. Just don't let it happen again."

Clare ducked her head and nodded sheepishly, then smiled at Anais. She pushed back the blankets and moved to one side of the bed. "If you're going to fall asleep watching over me, you might as well be comfortable. Get in here."

Anais hesitated, then took off her boots and climbed into the bed. Clare rolled onto her side and Anais turned her back. They spooned together under the blankets, and soon Clare was asleep with her hands linked over Anais' stomach.

Laikyn threw open the shades and Clare winced away from the sunlight. She didn't care what anyone said about comparative distance and atmosphere, the sun on Delene was brighter than the one she was used to. Especially in the mornings. She burrowed her face deeper into the pillow, the afterimage of Laikyn in her shorts and brassiere burned onto the back of her eyelids. The vision in question clambered onto the bed, covering Clare's body with her own and trying to draw her out with kisses on her neck, shoulders and the sliver of face that was accessible from her position. Clare burrowed deeper and rolled onto her stomach with a frustrated groan.

"Too early."

"Actually I let you sleep in." She blew away the feathers of hair that covered Clare's ear and licked the shell. Clare squirmed. "Come on. You have forty minutes to shower and dress and get to the Square."

Clare's voice was muffled against the bedclothes. "I have twenty minutes to sleep, then twenty minutes to splash myself with water, throw on enough clothes to look presentable, finish dressing on the Public Transpo, and prepare my apology for being five minutes late. Off-a me."

Laikyn sat up, straddling Clare's waist, and grabbed the straps of her tank top like she was settling in a saddle. "Come on. Up-up. Giddy up, horse." She reached back and swatted Clare's ass, and Clare lifted her head to yelp. Laikyn got one arm around her neck and pushed her hand into the scooped neck of Clare's shirt. "Wake up." She cupped Clare's right breast and, finding the nipple, pinched it.

"Oh!"

"There's more where that came from."

"You beast."

Laikyn growled. "I'll get you to shift on time if I have to drag you there with a leash. And if you're sore and rosy, then that will be your own fault."

Clare squirmed and bucked, trying to dismount her lover, but Laikyn tightened her thighs and held on. "I am a champion at this." She ground her hips against the curve of Clare's back. "Cry *anacol*."

"Never, sheila."

Laikyn twisted again, and Clare whimpered. "*Anacol*, you bitch."

"Good girl." She kissed Clare's hair above her ear and stroked the sore nipple with her thumb. "Did I hurt you badly?"

"Kiss it and make it better."

Laikyn chuckled. "Oh, but then we'd both be late."

"Then kiss me good morning, at least."

"That I can do." Laikyn winked and kissed the corner of Clare's mouth. Clare turned her head and their lips met, tongues twisting until Laikyn's grip on Clare's shirt relaxed.

Laikyn adjusted her position as Clare spread her legs apart. Laikyn settled neatly between them and shoved forward, continuing the kiss as she began to thrust against Clare. She curled her fingers on Clare's chest, her other hand following the curve of her spine and then sliding around the wrinkled track of her underwear's elastic. Clare arched her back to put some room between her and the mattress for her lover's hand.

"Oh, God, you're gonna make me so late," Laikyn moaned.

"Serves you right. Harder." She balled her fists in the sheets and pressed back to meet Laikyn's thrusts. Laikyn worked her agile fingers under the waistband of Clare's shorts and cupped her mound. They both moaned as Laikyn opened her with two fingers and dipped the third inside. "Laikyn..."

"There?"

"Yes."

Laikyn pressed her lips to Clare's neck and licked, and Clare came with a shudder and a cry. She reached back with one hand to repay the favor, and Laikyn guided the blindly searching fingers where she needed them to be. Clare turned, her cheek against the pillow, and watched as Laikyn thrust against her hand. After a few slow thrusts, Laikyn climaxed and fell on top of Clare. Clare flattened herself to the mattress, and Laikyn lazily kissed the back of her neck until she felt up to moving.

"You're a bad influence," Laikyn whispered, then kissed the back of Clare's neck.

Clare groaned. "I know. Now we're both going to be late."

Laikyn chuckled. "Actually, I lied. We have over an hour 'fore we have to leave."

Clare twisted, still trapped under Laikyn. "You wanker!"

"Nah, I lied so I wouldn't have to be a wanker." She bent down and kissed Clare. They were gearing up for a second round of distraction when Laikyn spanked her again. "But get up or we really will be late." She rolled to one side and slipped off the bed with far too much energy for the hour, and Clare remained tangled in the blankets for another few minutes enjoying the afterglow. When she heard the water running in the shower pipes, she finally roused herself and went to join Laikyn in the shower.

When Clare woke from the dream, she was aware of holding a body against hers, and the slow grind of her hips against her bedmate's posterior. She moved her hands to cup her partner's breasts, and twisted her head to lightly kiss her neck. The body in her arms squirmed, and hands circled around her wrist to gently guide it away. The spell was broken by a softly spoken, "Commander...?"

Her eyes opened and she pulled back immediately. "Anais. I'm so sorry."

"Don't be." Anais shifted on the bed and rolled onto her back. There was barely room in the bed for both of them, and Clare felt herself balanced precariously on the edge. She wasn't willing to cross the line between her and Anais, so she merely held herself where she was so she wouldn't fall. Anais ran her fingers through her sleep-mused hair, succeeding only in making it spikier, and said, "So I guess you had a pretty good dream, huh?"

"Yeah. Sorry again."

"Don't be. It was nice. I just didn't want you, um... doing anything you weren't... anything you didn't mean to be doing."

The silence loomed between them until they heard footsteps outside of the privacy curtain. Anais slipped out of bed and Clare was moving back into position as Dr. Monroe appeared at the foot of the bed. She took in the situation and tilted her head to one side.

"Oh. I could come back~"

"No. It's fine."

Anais gestured vaguely to someplace 'away.' "I have to relieve my relief anyway. Take care, Commander."

"You too. Thanks." She watched Anais go, then focused on Kali. "We were just sleeping."

"Uh-huh," Kali said. "How do you feel?"

Clare shrugged. "Headache. Weak." She moved her arms. "Still a little sore in the joints. But I'm not being digested by a Harvestman, so I'll spare you any complaints."

"Fair enough. You were oxygen deprived, which is to be expected. You woke up a few times over the past few days, but so briefly that I'm... you probably don't remember anything."

Clare shook her head, and Kali pointed at the chair.

"Anais was here ninety percent of the time. She wanted to be here as soon as you woke. I think she felt guilty."

"We went over that." Clare smiled and glanced at the bedside table, half-expecting to see a phial of oil. "Any other visitors?"

"No. Were you expecting anyone in particular?"

"No." She smoothed the blankets over her legs. "How long do I have to stay here?"

"Another twelve hours at the minimum. So I expect I'll be seeing your backside in eleven hours and fifty minutes." She raised an eyebrow, daring Clare to contradict her. When she remained silent, Kali addressed her tablet. "Captain and the command crew have been in a closed-doors meeting since you got back, talking about what to do now. Now that we know..." She gestured at the ceiling. "Harvestmen are back."

Clare shuddered. "And meaner than ever." A thought occurred to her. "Did... Nasim...?"

"We got him back, thanks to you. It will mean a lot to his family."

"There was a framed picture."

Kali's eyes brightened. "Yes! I completely forgot. We've all been tryin' to figure out what the hell it means. Why you bothered to save it above everything else."

"Something Laikyn said in her final message to me. It was the last message off the ship, and it was... postcard-trite. I think it wasn't meant for me. She wanted it to be seen, so someone might recognize it as a clue when they got aboard the ship." She shrugged. "She was just lucky I was the one who happened to be there."

Kali said, "So what does it mean? The picture? What was she trying to say?"

Clare shook her head. "I don't know. But I'm gonna find out."

Kali put her hand on Clare's ankle, symbolically shackling her to the bed. "In twelve hours, Commander. You can find out then."

"Eleven hours and fifty-five minutes. And counting."

Kali smiled and left Clare alone.

Articulate Right considered it his duty to inspect the shuttle used by the away team to escape the *Juno*. He was certain no one on the crew would blame him for requesting to stay behind. There was no such thing as cowardice when Harvestmen were involved. Still he felt he owed it to Nasim to be the one who cleaned up afterward. He wondered if he would have been the one to accompany Clare onto the Home level if he'd been on the mission. Would he have been the one lying dead in the infirmary? The thought made him shudder. There was no way of knowing if the mission would have gone differently if he was there, but he was fine with paying a small penance in order to quiet his guilty mind.

He moved toward the back of the ship to begin his search. It had been scanned upon approach but there were places where Harvestmen historically liked to hide because they were sensor blind spots. It was one reason they had been able to spread so completely across the galaxy. The damned things could be invisible if they...

His train of thought crashed to a stop when he saw the supply closet doors along the back wall. All the hatch doors were completely removable. At first glance it appeared the one on the right had simply been improperly replaced. It hung askew just a few centimeters. There was no reason to believe the worst, but the shuttle had come from a ship infested by Harvestmen. Sounding a false alarm was a better mistake than risking infiltration. He reached for his communicator but his hand never made contact. He looked down at the sharp, bloody line that now ended his arm just below the elbow and cold terror flooded through his body.

He turned and saw the Harvestman looming in the shuttle behind him, the scythe it used to cut off his arm still dripping blood. He couldn't draw breath or look away from the beast, so he was forced to watch as the bladed limb came down on the center of his head. He was grateful for the blood that washed over his eyes just before everything went dark. At least the image he took to his grave wouldn't be a monster.

XVI. LORELEI

Monsters don't make my books scary. It is when the monsters are chasing people with problems like yours or mine - bills or heartache or job stress - is when things start becoming truly frightening.
~ Zhenhua Je, horror writer

Dr. Monroe checked her watch with a rueful smile. "Twelve hours and one minute. You officers like proving me wrong, don't you?"

Clare smiled. "Actually, I just wanted to make sure you didn't drag me back down here for a check-up because I left early."

She had used the infirmary shower and was back in her uniform. She felt completely herself again, the haze of dissociation faded once she was back in the right clothing. Drifting between ships for what Kali told her was three hours and twenty-seven minutes felt like part of a dream now.

"Well, I have no reason to keep you. If you *wanted* to come back down here tomorrow so I could give you a once-over, I won't complain, but..."

"I think I'll pass, thanks." She started away from the bed, but she stopped. "Ah. While I was out, did I have any visitors besides Anais?"

Kali shook her head. "Not that I saw. Anais was pretty protective of you."

"She felt guilty."

"It's more than that." She smiled at Clare's confused look. "Oh, come on. She has it bad."

Clare shook her head. "She's a kid."

"She's twenty."

"That's a kid to me. She has a little crush, that's all. It's not real."

Kali's smile faded and she looked down at her hands. "You were lucky, Clare. You fell in love with your sister, so you didn't have to go through the whole secondary school nonsense. Crushes and romances and falling in love every five minutes. Do you know why they call them crushes? Because they almost always end with devastation. You don't know what it's like to love someone with your whole being and then have them dismiss you with a casual refusal. To have someone be your entire world, and then realize that you mean less than nothing to them... it... You didn't have to suffer like the rest of us did.

"I'm not saying Anais is in love with you, but you should keep in mind how real the feelings are when you let her down." She shrugged. "Hell, nothing's stopping you from throwing her a pity fuck."

Clare shifted uncomfortably. "It would mean too much."

"She might just have to go through the motions to move on. Just a quick roll in the hay to get it out of her system~"

"To me. It would mean too much to me." She coughed into her fist and reached up to adjust her headset. "I've never been with anyone else. I lost my virginity to Laikyn when we were both young, and we've always been together."

"Oh. I'm sorry. I didn't~"

"It's okay. You're friends with her, aren't you? Maybe you could mention that she needs to... set her sights elsewhere."

Kali shrugged. "It would be better coming from you."

Clare winced. "Can't you just put me back out in space for another four hours instead?"

Kali laughed and waved her away. "Don't leave her on the hook too long, Clare. The longer you wait, the harder it'll hit her."

"Yeah, yeah." She waved goodbye and left the infirmary. As if the Harvestmen weren't bad enough, now she had to deal with Anais' crush. She was starting to regret her rush to leave the safety of her hospital bed.

Clare was uneasy with the way the command crew gathered around her, welcoming her back into the fold. They were in the briefing room, and the picture she'd taken from Laikyn's room was sitting on the middle of the table like a centerpiece at a family dinner. Anais was at the far end of the room, and she smiled and waved sheepishly but didn't join the crush of officers around her.

Declan Hass, who had been brought onto the ship as a member of Nasim's regiment, had been given a cross-force battlefield promotion to the rank of Major in order to take command of his fellow Marines in his former CO's absence. He looked shaken, like a boy forced to dress up in Daddy's uniform for career day. Clare touched the insignia on his collar and she hugged him.

"You look good in a leaf, Dec."

"I'm just glad you're okay, Commander."

"You and me both." She stepped back and addressed the room. "So what did I miss?"

Lieutenant Commander Aleah Dodd, the head of the ship's Science department, stepped forward and picked up the drawing. "Finding this was a stroke of genius, Commander. Dr. Monroe mentioned you thought it was a message for anyone, but I wouldn't have even noticed it. No one here would have, either. I think Fate put you on that ship specifically so you could bring this back to us."

Captain Harp cleared his throat. "Lieutenant..."

"Right. Sorry. I just get so excitable." She turned the picture around and opened the frame. She lifted it out and held it up to reveal two circular depressions on the plastic. "This is where we found them. Microdiscs, sealed in protective wax. It's almost as if she knew you would have to take it out into space for a prolonged–"

Harp crossed his arms. "Without the karmic fate hokum, if you would?"

Dodd paused and lowered her head as she shifted gears. "Two discs, one marked with your name and identification number. Probably a private message, but we haven't watched it yet. We figured we'd leave that up to you, when you were able. The other one was more pertinent." She looked at Harp for his permission, and he gave the nod. She bent down over her station and began typing.

A holographic square with curved sides appeared above the table, the same image projected onto each plane so it could be seen from anywhere in the room. Laikyn's face was frozen on the screen, framed against the back wall of her quarters. She was in uniform, but her hair was down and curling around her face. Clare balled her hands into fists to dig her fingernails into her palms. Dodd pressed another key, and the image came to life.

"Lieutenant Commander Laikyn Prescott, linguist assigned to the PSV *Juno* making an... unauthorized report in the hopes someone will see if it this whole mess goes pear-shaped. Our crew has been drafted for a joint operation between Peaceful Sea and ACRA that our respective headquarters believe could result in an unstoppable weapon in future wars. They want to resurrect the Harvestmen. They hope we can change them, alter their behavior, make them... capitulate to us as their creator. They want us to try domesticating them."

Clare looked around, but it was obvious everyone else in the room had already heard the message. She should have noticed their unease, the pallor of disgust, but she was too nervous about being in a room full of people who had given her up for dead, however briefly, that she hadn't really paid attention to them.

Laikyn had continued. "~genetic samples they retrieved from previous attacks. Once we were well away from any habitable planets, out of the major shipping lanes, we grew a fucking Harvestman in our lab. It was restrained, it was isolated, and it was lobotomized so that it was basically just a shuffling, drooling thing, but ninety percent of the crew wouldn't go anywhere near it. We cut off its arms and~" She turned away and pressed the back of her hand to her lips until she could continue.

"We became butchers. I mean, sure, yeah, we created it. We grew the thing. It was just a science experiment, but it was a living creature. It painted." She laughed. "It drew these silly little pictures on the wall with its food. And it cried. You never want to hear a Harvestman cry. Eventually, we became naive. We thought it was a pet. People got comfortable with the idea of it being around, and our doctor went into the enclosure.

"We never found all the pieces of him. The Harvestman got out, and our Marines tracked it down and destroyed it." She leaned closer to the camera. "This was a limbless, defanged, half-brained abomination of a Harvestman, and it killed four of our men without breaking a sweat. When we examined the remains, we saw the true horror. An egg sac. We didn't know until that moment that we'd grown a female, and we've no idea how it got inseminated, but the fucking beastie was pregnant."

Laikyn looked down at her hands, which were now shaking. "Our respective Commands in ACRA and the PS, in their infinite idiocracy, have decided we should keep the eggs on hand. For study." She smiled ruefully. "It's too lucrative. The idea of having our own obedient army of Harvestmen is too sweet to pass up, so they want us to keep the eggs. It's my job to figure out how to talk to them when they hatch. Captain's hoping they'll imprint on us as parental figures. I think as smart as they are, they're still beasts. And those eggs in the infirmary are going to hatch our death.

"We're not supposed to speak of this to anyone off the ship. But I have to leave some kind of warning to anyone who comes after us. We know the Harvestmen are smart enough to clear away evidence of their presence, so I'm going to have to hide this somewhere innocuous and hope someone is smart enough to find it. I've sent Clare, my partner, a message and maybe that will make someone notice the painting. Anything more blatant and the Harvestmen will just destroy it.

"I've got to go. If they suspect I'm leaving this message, they'll force me to erase it and revoke my privileges. This ship has turned into a bloody internment camp. Everyone's paranoid. Everyone's scared, of the Harvestmen and of their commanding officers..." She ran her teeth over her bottom lip and rubbed the fingers of one hand over the knuckles of the other. "This is wrong. Everything happening on this ship right now is *wrong*. Please. Let it stop here."

The image stopped, and Clare felt like she had just snapped awake after a prolonged daydream. Day-nightmare, more accurately, and she shivered. The officers around her shifted their weight and looked at one another, then looked at Captain Harp.

"Well," he said. "At least we know the Harvestmen's rebirth started here. There's not another ghost ship out there waiting to be found."

Henderson Kite cleared his throat and said, "Not necessarily." Everyone looked at him and he shrugged apologetically. "I don't want to alarm anyone without reason, but how do we know that the *Prospekt* was the only ship to stumble over this science experiment? It's been two years since the *Juno* vanished. Granted, this is pretty much out on the raggedy edge, but there could have been other ships. And those ships could have been killed, and been found by other ships. And those ships..."

His voice trailed off.

Captain Harp took his seat and leaned forward with his elbows on the table. "So there's a good chance the Harvestmen infestation has just started all over again."

"Worse," Dr. Monroe said. "The first time they were just aliens who were fighting us because we were there. This time they've been engineered to be weapons. We turned them into killing machines and then we lost control of them."

Harp took off his glasses and laid them on the table. "Someone give me good news."

Major Hass touched his headset and his face, already graven, became stone. It looked as if he had aged ten years since Clare had last seen him, and he looked warily toward the captain.

"Go ahead, son."

"That was Chief Sheridan in the hangar. The crew that was cleaning the shuttle we brought over from the *Juno*, sir. Eight men, including Articulate Right, are missing. They've... apparently they've just vanished. Chief Sheridan says he found scratches on the deck plating."

Henderson Kite was the one to say what everyone else was thinking. "The Harvestmen are on board."

XVII. Tensions

Interspecies relationships are the final taboo. People have come to accept all manner of loving, consenting relationship bar that one. The general idea seems to be, "Love whoever makes you happy, but for your mother's sake, make it someone from the same basic DNA." The subculture of interspecies lovers (or xenophiles, as they're starting to be called) came to mainstream attention when Captain Una Sarch married the holographic representation of his Personal Assistance Matrix.
~ introduction to *Mom, I'm Marrying an Energy Cloud*, by Dr. Philipe Arbanel and Eoem Arbanel

The ship was immediately placed on high alert. Sergeant Kite suggested making their situation known, but Harp was still wary of causing undue panic. Clare said, "Sir. With all due respect, this could be happening to multiple ships across this sector. At the very least we should provide a warning to approach any derelict vessel with caution."

Major Hass said, "I agree. Playing the cards close to our vest would only benefit the Harvestmen and make it easier for them to gain footholds. If someone had warned us about the *Prospekt*, things may have gone differently for us both there and here."

Harp considered their proposals, but refused to budge. "If the

Peaceful Sea goes on alert, ACRA is going to want to know why. If we tell them... we all remember what happened last time ACRA got involved with Harvestmen. Ms. Gray, have you prepared that message for the worst case scenario?"

"Aye, sir."

"Excellent. Follow Lieutenant Colonel Prescott's lead and disguise it so the bastards don't recognize it as a warning when they're cleaning house."

Kira, obviously shaken to have a task covering the eventuality everyone on board would be gruesomely murdered, nodded. "Aye, sir."

"Sergeant Kite, Lieutenant... sorry. Major Hass. I want you to coordinate your teams and do a level-by-level sweep of this ship. We have to assume a Harvestman did get onboard via the shuttle we brought back from the *Juno*. I want it found, and I want it destroyed."

"Aye sir," both men said.

"The rest of you... once we find the damned thing, we're going to be going non-stop for as long as it takes to track any vessels that may have come this way and gotten infested themselves. If one ship infested two others, and..." He sighed. "We could have a very long time until we're able to rest again, so I want you to take full advantage of it. I need you relaxed for what is to come."

Sadiq Malki shook his head. "Sir, I'm not going to just sit on my ass and nap while we're searching this ship for a Harvestman."

"You'll follow orders, Engineer. But if you need a reason to do so, do it for your men. They'll need you to be on top of your game when the shit goes down."

Sadiq reluctantly nodded and glanced at Hass.

Harp dismissed them. "All right. You have your orders. Keep your comms close."

The group dispersed, and Clare paused at the door. When everyone had gone, she turned and walked back to the Captain, who had hesitated at the table with his back to the doors.

"Sir."

"You have your orders, Commander. I don't care if you spent the last few days in the infirmary–"

"Yes, sir. I'm about to take your order right now, but something occurred to me. I just wanted to run it by you while we were alone."

He nodded but didn't turn to face her. "Go ahead."

"It's fortunate we took the charter to pick up Thetis:scholar.

Considering how far out of the way Leucothea is, and how unusual it is for us to take such a mission. I was amazed that the Regent was able to pay enough to make it worth our while. But now I'm starting to wonder if we had an alternative purpose in taking the commission. I wonder if you were ordered to manufacture a reason to come out into this area and it just took you a while to find a plausible excuse."

Harp turned slightly, giving her his profile. "And what have you determined, Commander?"

"Did you know about this experiment?"

"Would it matter if I did?"

"As your second in command, I would be offended you didn't warn me about it if you did. Sir."

Harp walked to the window. "You have your orders, Commander Cossin. I suggest you follow them. We're about to get very busy."

"Aye. Sir."

She started to leave, but he spoke again. "It was because of the ship..." She waited nearly a minute before he spoke again. "The *Juno*. It was because the *Juno* was the missing ship that I accepted the assignment, and it was for the same reason I refrained from telling you about it. I hoped to the Power that they were wrong. Hell, I hoped it had gotten sucked into a black hole rather than... I'm sorry, Commander. You deserved to know. But I honestly couldn't bring myself to be the one who told you."

Clare blinked her eyes dry, her back to her captain. "Will that be all, sir?"

"Yes."

She left him standing alone at the window, hands behind his back, glaring out at the empty space around them.

Thetis opened the door to her quarters and smiled warily. "Commander. I'm glad you are here. The alarms have been sounding, but no one will tell us why."

"Just stay in your quarters and you should be fine. May I come in?"

"Certainly." She stepped aside, gathering her robes so Clare wouldn't tread on them, and let the door close behind her. The room was even more of a shrine now, and Thetis noticed Clare examining the changes. "Don't worry. I will undo all of this before I depart. But since the ship's estimated arrival at my destination seems to be ever-increasing~"

"It's fine. You deserve to be comfortable." She turned and faced Thetis. "Why didn't you come to visit me? In the infirmary, after I got back."

"I did. But your friend, Anais, was already there. I assumed she had your vigil well in hand, so I left her to it. I did not mean to offend you."

Clare shook her head. "I'm not offended." She looked around the quarters and then sat on the edge of the bed. Thetis moved closer. "I don't know what I am. I'm scared. I'm hurt. Not by you, by..." She pressed her fingers to her forehead and rubbed in slow circles. Thetis stepped closer and gently moved Clare's hand, replacing the fingers with her own. Clare sighed, and Thetis used her other hand on Clare's temple. "Thank you."

Thetis sat beside Clare without ceasing her ministrations, and Clare was soon lulled into a serene, peaceful state. She turned to face Thetis, aware of her moving closer but unwilling to pull back. She parted her lips in anticipation of a kiss, but Thetis surprised her by moving her head to one side until her cheek grazed Clare's. Thetis' skin was cool, and Clare turned her head to increase the pressure, her hand moving to Thetis' hip as Thetis pushed both hands into Clare's hair. She tangled her fingers with the short strands, and Clare closed her eyes and sagged into the other woman's embrace. A hug. A simple hug. She smiled at how mundane it was, and how great it felt to just be held. Thetis' face was like thick spider webs against her face, but she didn't care. Her mind swam, and Thetis' robes wrinkled under her fingers as they tightened over her hip. Her mind raced.

Laikyn brings her yellow flowers. Laikyn's fingers run slowly down her back, waking her. Laikyn wears a black skirt that swishes around her thighs when she moves. Laikyn whispers words against Clare's mouth as they kiss. Tongue in mouth. Hands under clothing where it's warmer. Undressed. Weight on her. Laikyn between her legs. Laikyn on top of her, straddles her face, Clare's cheeks framed by warm thighs that she turns to kiss. Clare drops her hand to Laikyn's lap in the lecture hall. Fingers her to a silent orgasm; Laikyn's fingers grip the edge of the desk until her knuckles are white. Laikyn in a Gender Suit, Clare's tongue running over flat chest and hard abdomen until she reaches Laikyn's rented erection and takes it in her mouth. Clare pressing against the vibrating edge of a shuttle's hull for a galactic orgasm. In the shower with her fingers, her cries echoing on the tile. Clenching around two of Laikyn's fingers, or around Laikyn's tongue, or closing her thighs around Laikyn's foot.

Clare pulled away from Thetis with a sharp intake of breath, her eyes flashing open as she came back to herself. Thetis rolled back as well, her eyes half-lidded, swaying like a drunk about to pass out in the gutter. Her cheeks had a violet hue, and her hair was a darker shade of white-blue than normal.

"I apologize," Thetis gasped. She blinked and turned her head, gathering her robes to cover her chest and turning her knees outward. "I did not even know if that was possible with a human. I shouldn't have done it."

"Done what?" She was still breathless.

"I just made love to you. I am terribly sorry, Commander. If I had known it was possible... I only wished to comfort you, to set your mind at ease..."

Clare swallowed and furrowed her brow. "It's okay."

"No. It's not."

Clare touched Thetis' shoulder and leaned in to kiss her cheek. Thetis tensed, but then turned her head and their lips grazed against each other. Clare parted her lips, and Thetis pushed her tongue between them. It was flat and textured, almost like sucking on a leaf, and Clare furrowed her brow to get over the initial unease the initial comparison gave her. She moved her hand up Thetis' side, suddenly desperately curious to discover just how different a Leucothean body was from a human.

Her communicator sounded, and Clare pulled back. "That could be one of the search teams." Thetis touched her lips and stood up, turning her back to Clare as she checked the call. "I should... go. I should check this out."

"Yes. I think that would be for the best."

"Thetis..."

She turned and smiled sheepishly. "I'm not ashamed. But I do not believe pursuing what just happened any further would be of benefit to either of us. Go, please."

Clare nodded. "Thank you." She didn't know if she was grateful for the 'love-making,' the kiss, or the excuse to escape, but she knew it needed to be said. "I'll come back when things have settled down." Thetis nodded, and Clare left the rooms.

The call had originated in the Crow's Nest, so Clare ascended the steep stairs to Anais' small kingdom. The leather chair was empty and spun toward the entrance so that Clare could see the seat. Anais was standing off to one side, eyes on the screens, but she turned at the sound of Clare's approach and smiled nervously.

"Hi, Commander."

"Anais. Is everything okay? Did you spot something?"

"No. Captain Harp asked me to keep my eyes out for any other ships, but we're all alone out here." She stepped closer and said, "I called you up here because of his other order. To take advantage of the security team's search time to rest up. But I never sleep, and I can't imagine sleeping under the circumstances, and I'm just going crazy up here alone, so I thought what better way to spend this time than doing something I may never get a chance to do again?"

Clare tensed. "Anais, I think~"

"Shut up... please." She winced and moved closer. "I feel like a shit for doing this now. I mean, your girlfriend..." She looked at the window and quickly looked away. "I've had a crush on you since I joined up, Commander. You were taken, so I was content to just admire you from afar. But now, we have fucking Harvestmen on the ship and..." Her eyes welled up. "If I have to die, I just want to kiss you. Can I just kiss you and we can leave it at that?"

Clare stood silent for a long moment, then closed the distance between them in a single step. She cupped Anais' face, and Anais made a strangled noise of relief before her lips were covered. Clare closed her eyes when she felt the human tongue against her lips, and her arm slid around Anais' waist to flatten against the curve of her ass. *This* felt right... this felt normal. She pulled back and kissed Anais' bottom lip.

"Oh, wow."

"Still want to leave it at that?"

Anais opened her eyes and searched Clare's face, then shook her head. "No, ma'am."

Clare bent forward and they kissed again. This time she was the aggressor, guiding Anais back until her legs touched the seat of her chair. She moved one hand up and undid the buttons of Anais' waistcoat, helping the girl shrug out of it before guiding her down into the chair. She braced her hands on the back of the chair and stared into Anais' eyes, wide with hope and desire.

"This isn't because we might die, and it's not because of what happened on the *Juno*. It's happening because I want you."

Anais smiled. "Good."

Clare kissed her and climbed onto the chair, her knees tucked in tight on either side of Anais' hips. The chair tipped back, and they continued the kiss for as long as possible before they began helping each other undress. When Anais lifted her arms to allow Clare to take off her shirt, Clare ran her hands over the comfortingly familiar pink flesh, her fingers slipping into one cup of her brassiere to tease her nipple, and decided this was exactly what she needed to take her mind off the past few days.

"You'll be the first person I've ever... the second person I've *ever*..."

"Sh." Anais put two fingers on Clare's mouth and let her moisten them with her tongue. "I'll try to be worthy of the honor."

Clare kissed Anais again and pressed against her. Anais gripped the material of Clare's jerkin with both hands and sank back into her chair, ignoring the protest of its springs as it took both their weights.

CHAPTER FIVE

XVIII. SEARCH

...approaching is currently under high alert. Ship identified as Paralus is under attack. Please be advised to keep your distance. Should assistance be required, an automated system will issue a distress call. The vessel you are approaching is currently under high alert. Please be advised...
~ automatic override message replacing standard ship IDEC

Every Marine onboard was called to duty and geared up with Fore-Arms and armored uniforms. They wore helmets with faceplates onto which they could project blueprints of the ship and read heat signatures through the hull. Major Declan Hass and Sergeant Henderson Kite were in charge of the search parties. Kite served as commander of the on-ship security, while Hass was now fulfilling Nasim's role as commanding officer for the ship's contingent of Marines. He stood uneasy in front of the ranks, trying to hide just how nervous he was. Kite saw through him and took him aside.

"It's a hell of a thing for your first official action, but those men are counting on you, Major. You're not one of them anymore, you're their leader."

"I'm sure it means a lot to them. I'm not even one of them."

"Right. You know why Captain Harp picked you to take Nasim's place? Because it's what Nasim wanted. He asked for you to be his replacement in the worst case scenario. He trusted you. Now you just gotta trust yourself."

"We're saying that a lot. 'Worst case scenario.'"

"If this doesn't count, then I'd hate to see what does."

Declan took a steadying breath and nodded his gratitude before stepping back out in front of the men. "I want six-man teams sweeping each deck. The advance team will consist of two men doing the searching while a third watches their backs. Once they're clear, the back-up team will come in behind them. When everyone has been through, lock down the level and go *back*. We have enough people to cover the ship, so you only have to worry about your particular deck. Leave no stone unturned and no door closed. This thing got on board by hiding in a closet just barely big enough to fit into. Think about that when you're looking for the motherfucker."

Kite said, "This is a Harvestman. Think of every campfire story, every nightmare, and every tall tale told in a bar and assume every single one of them is true. You've heard of take no prisoners? Shoot at anything that skitters or hisses. Worst case scenario, we'll have to apologize to Ensign Garcia for killing her cat."

This was greeted by quiet laughter from the gathered forces.

"All right, everyone. None of our people dies today. Let's get out there and hunt down this Harvestbastard."

The soldiers moved out, splitting into six-person teams as ordered. Declan and Kite stood against the wall to guide them toward the lifts with individual orders for which deck would be their responsibility. Once all the decks were taken, Declan sent a few soldiers to the bridge and twelve were sent to take the hangar. The hall was finally empty, and Declan checked the charge on his Fore-Arm.

"I'll take the hangar. It's where the thing got onto the ship, so maybe it's hanging around."

"You're taking the bridge. It's your station, Major."

Declan looked like a grammar school student who had just been told he couldn't go out for recess. "Sir..."

"Gunny Nasim went on every away mission and led his troops into battle, blah blah blah. He also had a file full of recriminations, suspensions, and official reprimands. He was never going to get promoted, but he didn't care so long as he was on the front lines.

You and your boyfriend want to start a family eventually, you keep your nose clean. One day you'll be transferred somewhere safe. Right now, your place is on the bridge. Your people need you there."

Declan wanted to argue, but everything Kite had said was the truth. He nodded begrudgingly and said, "Aye, sir."

"I'm not a sir to you anymore, Major. Let's go." He stepped around Declan and went to the lift. A few seconds later, Declan pushed away from the wall and joined him.

The crew and passengers were confined to quarters, but no one was unwilling to allow their rooms to be searched. The sensors in their helmets were set to pick up the unfathomably low body heat the new breed of Harvestmen put off, so it wasn't necessary to tear apart the walls of every room to make sure the castaway wasn't hiding in them. Once the soldiers figured out how to differentiate between the low heat of a Harvestman and the low heat of everyday inanimate objects, the search moved faster.

Ensign Ethan Cobb ascended the stairs that led to the Crow's Nest and stuck his head inside. Commander Cossin was seated in the Navigator's chair, with Anais draped across her lap. Anais' head was on the Commander's shoulder, apparently asleep, and both women seemed to be naked underneath the clothes draped over Anais' body. The light from the monitors reflected off their sweat, and Commander Cossin slowly turned her head toward the door when she realized he was there.

"We're fine up here, Ensign." Though she spoke softly, Anais stirred in her arms.

"Yes, ma'am. Sorry, ma'am." He heard the spring of the chair protest under shifting weight as he retreated to search elsewhere.

On the bridge, Declan relayed information from his teams to Captain Harp. "Decks 1 through 7 are clear, sir. Awaiting official reports from Decks 8 through 12. The team in the hangar reports more evidence of the Harvestman's passage, but no sign of the creature itself."

"Thank you, Major."

Kira left her station and stood near Hass. "Captain, I have a suggestion as to how we may narrow down the search. Harvestmen are quiet when they move, but it's impossible for them to be completely silent. If I can get close enough, I think I could hear it. When they attacked our planet, they never attempted stealth tactics because they knew it would be pointless."

Clare arrived in the bridge, her hair mussed and her uniform waistcoat unbuttoned. She had heard the end of Kira's suggestion. "Not without a security detail. I'll head it up myself, sir, with your permission."

Harp considered it and then nodded. "Major Hass, you and Commander Cossin will provide protection. Ms. Gray, you are to listen and point out sources of noise. Do not under any circumstance confront the beast yourself."

Kira smiled nervously. "You don't have to make that an order, sir." She turned slightly toward Clare and tilted her head to the side. She smelled the air and smiled. "I'm sure I would be in capable hands with Major Hass, if you would like to continue resting, ma'am."

Clare narrowed her eyes. "I'm plenty rested."

"Hm. Good for you."

Declan frowned, but Clare gave him a sharp shake of her head to tell him not to ask. "We'll start on the levels already cleared. If the Harvestman is as clever as the others have been acting, it may have backtracked. And I want you to be armed."

Kira shook her head. "I won't risk shooting someone."

"Take the gun," Declan said. "If you have to use it, everyone around you will probably already be dead anyway."

"That's not exactly comforting." Kira took the gun offered to her by Ensign Platt, and stuck it under her uniform belt. "Okay. Sooner gone, sooner done."

Captain Harp stood. "Good luck, Commander."

"Thank you, Captain," Clare said.

When they were in the lift, Kira said, "Has something occurred between you and Captain Harp? Your tone with him just now was... unusual."

"Everything's fine," Clare said. "Just drop it."

Kira inhaled and held her hands in front of her. She smiled slightly. "Navigator Quimby's perfume smells good on you, Commander."

"Drop that, too."

Declan said, "Do I need to understand any of what you're talking about?"

"No."

"Okay, good. I'll just keep Ms. Gray alive so you can continue having your cryptic little conversations with one another."

Kira snickered and, despite herself, Clare smiled as well. Declan called ahead to let the security team know they were en route to Deck 1, and an escort was waiting for them when the doors opened. Corporal Greene said, "We've been over this deck thrice, and no sign of the Harvestman. More than happy to let Ms. Gray give it a whirl, though."

Declan nodded. "Tell your men to stand where they are. I don't want any more noise than necessary."

"Aye, sir." He touched his headset. "Team, stand-down. Remain where you are. Keep your noise to a minimum."

Kira took a deep breath. Clare put a hand on her arm. "Are you ready?"

"As I'll ever be." She slid her foot across the deck without lifting it. Clare found the unnatural quiet to be overwhelming; a part of her insisted she say something just to break the silence, but she refrained. Kira's ears were wide open, and any extraneous noise would likely harm her. So Clare stayed quiet and slid her feet along the deck in Kira's wake. She kept her arms slightly away from her sides, both Fore-Arms charged and ready in case the Harvestman made an appearance.

It took them nearly ten minutes to reach the opposite end of the deck, and Kira pressed her lips together. "No. Nothing here."

Declan took the opportunity to speak. "Teams up to Deck 12 are reporting no sign of the Harvestman."

Clare said, "You didn't smell anything?"

"A faint rotten smell, but it was very faded. The Harvestman may have passed through this deck to get somewhere else, but it was a brief interval."

Declan said, "It would have to go through here from the hangar if it wanted to get to the interior of the ship."

Clare nodded. "Okay. On to the next deck, Dec."

They continued their slow progress on the next three decks, with Kira reporting only the faintest traces of the Harvestman's passage. They were just starting on Deck 5 when Declan touched his earpiece and made a hand signal for the women to wait. Clare put a hand on Kira's upper arm, and she stopped.

"Where are you?" Declan asked. "Okay. I'll be right there." To Clare, he said, "Sergeant Kite is on Deck 18. He says there's something I need to see. You might as well come along."

Kira said, "You can leave me with these soldiers. I'll continue the search."

"You're certain you'll be okay?"

Kira smiled. "I'll be surrounded by Marines and security personnel. I'll be the safest person on this damn ship. Go. I'll be fine."

Clare nodded and followed Declan back to the lift. When they were alone, Clare asked, "How did Kite sound?"

"Nervous."

"Great," Clare murmured.

When they arrived on Deck 18, they didn't have to search for the reason they had been called. Kite was standing near the lift, and a group of Marines had surrounded an area nearby. Kite's eyes were white, and his posture was rigid. "Commander. I'm glad you came. We have a problem."

"Add it to the pile," she said.

Kite led her to the reason for his call, and Clare felt a chill. An access hatch had been pried open, the metal twisted and torn with what must have required immense strength. Inside there was an incredibly narrow space that Clare doubted she could have fit into, let alone a full-grown Harvestman. Whichever soldier had checked it out was definitely going above and beyond, but it had paid off.

The smell of rotting flesh rose up from within, and a green slime coated the surface of the crawlspace. The green slime was of secondary concern.

Kite bent down and picked up one of the jagged shards that had been embedded in the slime. He turned it over in the light and held it out so Clare could get a better look. She ignored the stench and leaned closer.

"I've never seen one, so someone will have to confirm it, but--"

"It's a Harvestman egg. A hatched egg." She looked down at the remaining pieces and estimated at least seven eggs had been in the sludge.

"Great," Declan said.

"Oh, that's not the worst part," Kite said. He dropped the shard and wiped the ooze off his glove with a handkerchief that he then dropped into the opening. "Harvestmen are born hungry, and their females are impregnated not long after."

Clare counted the egg remnants again, as if knowing there were only five instead of seven would make any difference at all. One, five, seven, twenty-four. The numbers didn't matter. The Harvestmen were in the *Paralus*, they were evading capture, and the dumb humans couldn't even find one.

"We're not going to beat them."

Kite used his boot to push the twisted hatch back into place. "Yeah. I'm about this close to suggesting the captain cut life support and open this place up to the vacuum."

"It wouldn't work," Clare said. "The Harvestmen can survive in a vacuum."

Kite shook his head. "Not for them. For us. It'd be a damn sight more humane than what these beasties will do to us."

Clare watched him walk away and looked down at the misshapen hatch. There was a chance he was right, and the *Paralus* was doomed. If that was true, maybe they should stop wasting time on defense and start planning how they would warn the next ship to stay the hell away.

XIX. DESPAIR

The body count attributed to the Harvestmen doesn't even scratch the surface of the people who truly lost their lives to these things. Yes, the Harvestmen slashed, chewed, devoured a great number of people and their victims number in the thousands. But that number pales in comparison to the number who, in the face of an unstoppable and insatiable enemy, simply gave up and took their own lives. The Harvestmen have the blood of those people on their heads as well.
~ President of ACRA, post Final Attrition

Captain Harp sounded defeated when he spoke over the tannoy. Science Officer Aleah Dodd sat on her bed, legs crossed in front of her with the feet tucked into her bent knees. She was crying. She wasn't the sort to get depressed, to be pessimistic, but she remembered the news reports. She had seen the footage of worlds devastated by the Harvestmen. And these were even *worse* monsters? Science, the doctrine to which she had devoted her life, had let these things loose on the universe again.

Eight eggs. That made nine Harvestmen on board, more if they didn't find the newborns before they were impregnated and gave birth. She was trembling, and tears dripped off her chin as she lifted her gun. It was humane. Compared to what the Harvestmen would do to her, it was the most humane way to go. Her death was imminent either way. At least this way it wouldn't hurt for long.

She killed herself just as Captain Harp's message began to repeat.

After discovering the hatched eggs, the command crew returned to the briefing room to take stock and consider a new course of action. Something began nagging at Clare during the lift ride, and she nurtured the quiet voice until it had formed what it was trying to say. When the staff was gathered, Henderson Kite was the first to speak.

"Sir, as much as I hate to be the one to suggest this, we have only one course of action. We cannot risk weaponized Harvestmen getting loose on a civilized world. As we've already seen, they are smart enough to castaway to get onto new ships, so we can't evacuate. Even if the lifeboats were a viable option, we'd have to take apart each one to make sure no Harvestmen were hiding in the closets. By the time we were done, they'll have taken over the ship. We have to sacrifice ourselves, sir."

"The hell with that," Sadiq said.

"We're all dead anyway. No matter what happens in the next few days, our heads are on the chopping block. I say we take the bastards out with us. Send a warning on the strongest frequency we can find telling people what happened and then make peace with whoever we worship. It's the only realistic option."

Anais joined them, pale and trembling. Clare went to her, and Anais clung to her for support. "Anais? What happened? What's wrong?"

"Aleah Dodd killed herself. I was trying to get her on the headset, to get her here. She didn't answer, so I thought the Harvestmen..." She sniffled. "I called the Marines on the Home level to check her rooms and they found her. She shot herself."

Kite said, "It's beginning. Once people hear the Harvestmen are on board, it's wait to be eaten or take the quick way out." He formed a pistol with two fingers and pressed it to his temple. "I'm not suicidal. Believe me, I'm as kill-or-be-killed as the next person. But that's not an option with the Harvestmen. ACRA going after them wasn't called a war because you can't war with an animal no matter how smart it is. They had to be eradicated. And, I'm sorry, but we can't do that without taking ourselves with them."

Clare whispered, "Wax in my ears."

Everyone looked at her. "Pardon?" Captain Harp said.

She didn't realize she had spoken aloud, and even now wasn't sure what she had said. "Sorry, sir. I was just thinking out loud."

"About wax in your ears?"

"It was the last message sent from the *Juno*. Laikyn sent it to me. It was a clue to look behind the drawing, but what if it served another purpose. Laikyn was a linguist, so she liked playing games with her messages. Sometimes a birthday card could be a cryptic message, or a note that said she was going to pick up supplies was a love letter. In her message she said there were sirens on the shoreline and she had wax in her ears."

"It's from an ancient tale," Radka said. "Ulysses had his men seal their ears with wax so they couldn't hear the sirens and be tempted to their deaths."

Clare furrowed her brow. "At the time, I thought it was just... playful. But now that I know what was happening aboard the ship, I think the entire thing was a code. I think it's a clue to how we can stop the bastards. Radka, what else do you know about the story?"

Radka tensed, obviously wishing she hadn't spoken up. "The ship had to pass some dangerous sirens, whose song made rational thought impossible. Sailors would leap to their deaths to try and swim to them."

"Sirens were inescapable death," Declan said. "Like Harvestmen. But where does wax come in? They always attack silently. They don't have a song."

Clare said, "Who checked my EVA suit when I got back from my excursion?"

"Sergeant Odon," Declan said.

"Did he find out why the radio stopped working?"

"Not really. He said something overloaded the processors."

Clare said, "She melted my ears. When I went into Laikyn's quarters, she must have had something set up to do that."

Harp said, "But why on Earth would she endanger you like that?"

"She wouldn't have. Laikyn would never draw me somewhere and then purposefully put me into danger. So I have to assume that it was an attempt to keep me safe."

"How does being deaf and mute on a derelict spaceship keep you safe?" Kite asked.

Clare blindly scanned the room as her mind worked. "Derelict. It was a derelict spacecraft." Her eyes widened. "How did the Harvestmen find us?"

"Which time?"

"Either time. On the *Prospekt* they were hibernating. We assumed one of them was keeping lookout and alerted the others. But on the *Juno*, Nasim and I were on the Home level. We were two people on a ship designed for hundreds. How did it know exactly where to find us? On both ships, the Harvestmen always knew exactly where we were in order to cut us off from escape."

Kira said, "You think they were listening to your radio signals."

"Or maybe they were just aware of the radio signals being broadcast. They pick up on a little bit of static and they follow it back to the source."

Declan said, "Shouldn't Nasim's radio have been affected as well?"

"I have no idea where in the room Laikyn would have put her... whatever the fuck it was that melted my radio. But it didn't matter because Nasim stayed in the doorway until he died. Then I was dragging him through the room." She racked her brain trying to remember anything out of the ordinary, any electric shock or sense of discomfort. "The point is, she had to have a reason for doing it. I think somehow the Harvestmen home in on radio signals."

"Even if that's true," Declan said, "how can we use that to our advantage? If we tell everyone to stop using their radios, our security teams and our passengers will all be sitting ducks. We'll be asking people to cut themselves off from reinforcements."

"We'll have to move fast," Kite said. Now that he'd been given an alternative, he seemed eager to backtrack from his suggestion of mass suicide. "We recall our forces and get them into a single area of the ship, and everyone else..."

Clare said, "They should be secure in their quarters. The Harvestmen couldn't get into Laikyn's quarters on the *Juno* once the doors closed."

Kali said, "People will panic. I'd like to offer sedatives to those who want them before we go into lockdown."

Harp nodded. "I'll let people know they're available." He looked at Clare. "What do you propose we do once our people are gathered and safe?"

"God, I don't know. This isn't a plan, sir."

Declan said, "If they do lock onto radio signals, we can use that against them. Harvestmen are mostly blind. We cut off all radio, then turn one back on. They'll be drawn to it like moths to a flame. It's how they reacted when we brought new radios onto the *Prospekt* and the *Juno*. They'll swarm the signal."

Harp spoke up. "We'll draw them into the hangar. It can become a closed environment. We just have to make sure we get all the bastards in one go. I don't want any eggs being left behind on my ship."

"There's a chance they won't fall for this," Clare said. "Harvestmen can never be called stupid, and these were designed to fight armies. They'll have to be expecting some sort of tactic. The odds they'll fall for a single stationary radio left in a vulnerable location~"

Harp said, "It won't be a stationary signal. We'll have to convince them that everyone else got off the ship somehow and there's one person left behind to exterminate them."

Kite and Declan both said, "I'll do it."

"No, you won't. As Commander Cossin already deduced, we're in this mess because of me. I'll be the one to draw the Harvestmen into the hangar."

"All due respect, sir, the hell you will." Clare stepped away from Anais.

Harp looked at her. "What do you suggest, Commander, we draw straws? I've already lost too many crew members because I agreed to take this mission. I won't risk anyone else. No sense in wasting any more time and letting any more of these things give birth. Kira, get on the tannoy and let everyone know what we're planning. I want these motherfuckers off my ship even if I have to lead them out myself."

XX. Silence

The idea of a captain going down with his ship is misleading. A captain uses his last breath to save his ship and her passengers, but if he can save them by sacrificing himself, then that is what he must do. Sometimes the captain goes down so the ship can go on.
~ suicide note, Captain Elmer Scarborough of the British Rule Vessel *Warwick* who fled in a shuttle while his ship was under fire on a kamikaze mission to destroy an ACRA vessel

Clare watched Captain Harp as he typed something onto his tablet, unsure of what to say. Finally he finished typing and looked at her, and she realized she had to say something. "Laikyn was always a wordsmith, sir. She may have just been waxing lyrical in her note. Probably doesn't mean anything after all."

He smiled and stepped around his desk. "Do you believe that, Clare?"

"I can believe a lot of things, sir."

"I believe that if we don't take this admittedly sketchy theory, we all might as well follow Ms. Dodd's example and discharge our weapons backward. This is a good theory. I'm willing to give my life to test it, so you can be damn sure I believe in it." He put his hands on her shoulders and squeezed. "Keep the ship safe, Captain

Cossin."

She tensed and lowered her head. "Acting-Captain. And sir... I don't~"

"Someone has to do it, and I've already promoted Declan once today. If I do it again, he might get a swelled head."

Clare smiled. "He'd make Admiral by month's end."

Harp chuckled. "Come on. Our people have been scared long enough. Let's go get the boogeyman." He led her out of his office to find the rest of the staff was waiting. "What have you come up with?"

Declan looked at Kite, who stepped forward. "You'll lead the Harvestmen into the hangar bay. You'll take shelter in one of the shuttles while you let the creatures surround you. Once you're certain they're all in the room with you, give us the signal by powering up. That will cause an alert on the bridge, since the hangar doors will be closed."

"And once we get that signal," Declan said, "we'll activate the biohazard protocols." His voice broke on the last word. The protocols would flood the hangar with chemicals that would destroy anything organic. It was a failsafe to prevent the spread of alien diseases and contagion, but the PSV *Artemis* had discovered the hard way that it worked splendidly on human and Terepian flesh. Experiments after the Attritions ended showed it was effective on Harvestman flesh as well.

Harp nodded and looked at his staff. "Well. I suppose saying anything else now would just be grandiose. It's been an honor to serve with you all. Captain Rani Clare Cossin, as of now, you have command of the *Paralus*."

"It's my honor. I'll treat her well for you, sir."

He smiled and winked, then looked at his people again. "Ms. Gray?"

"Radios have all been silenced, sir, and the civilians have locked themselves away. The last unit of Marines and security officers are returning to the command levels now."

"Well done. Sergeant Kite, keep an eye out for my signal. I don't want those things surrounding me any longer than necessary. Understood?"

"Aye, sir."

Clare said, "Attention." Every officer snapped their boots together and raised a flat hand to their brows. Harp nodded and returned the salutes, then looked at Clare. "Sorry, Captain."

"Don't be, sir. You gave me a chance to say goodbye."

"Nearly got you killed, too."

"Worth it."

He winked at her again and stepped forward. "Ms. Gray, I'll need a radio. How long will it take for the Harvestmen to come after me?" He took the radio from her and checked the settings. He was also wearing Fore-Arms for the first time since being a Commander. He adjusted them slightly so they were a little more comfortable and then said, "Captain Cossin."

"...yes, sir?"

"Please lower your weapon." He half-turned to look at her over his shoulder. Her Fore-Arm was aimed at the back of his head, the barrel glowing red.

"I..." She dropped her arm. "It was on stun."

"I know."

"I had to try, sir. We can still think of another way."

"Do you honestly think there's another way?"

She refused to answer.

"I appreciate what you were thinking, but this is my cross to bear, understood?"

"Aye, sir."

Declan coughed. "Uh. To answer your question, sir, we've been radio silent for nearly five minutes now. The Harvestmen should be confused. Once another radio starts up, I think they'll be plenty interested in what's going on. If Comma~ Captain Cossin is correct, then they'll be on you faster than you'll like."

Harp nodded. "Then I suppose I should get going. I wish I'd taken a few more athletics courses the past few years." He patted his stomach and nodded. "If this doesn't work, find another way to save my ship. Barring that... give her a good sendoff."

"Aye, sir," Clare said.

He turned and walked out of the briefing room. Clare resisted the urge to tackle him, cripple him somehow, even though she knew he would never forgive her for it. They followed him as far as the bridge before breaking off to their own stations. Clare eyed his seat and decided to remain standing out of respect for him, clasping her hands behind her back as Anais left the bridge to take her place in the Crow's Nest. She returned less than ninety seconds later.

"Still no Harvestman life signs registering anywhere on the ship."

Kite said, "Maybe they got bored and left."

Clare smiled. "We can only hope."

"The Captain's radio just went active," Kira reported. She had taken off her headset and the lines around her mouth were deeper than usual at the pain of hearing everything. "Two decks below us, moving toward the hangar."

"Do you hear anything else? Sounds of pursuit?"

Kira tilted her head to the side, then tensed. "Yes. They're moving. Laikyn was right, Captain."

Clare was thrown by the use of rank, but she shook it off. "How many do you think there are?"

The question wasn't directed to anyone in particular, and it was Declan who answered. "No more than ten. Only one was pregnant, and it gave birth... the others will need a few hours before they're ready to lay eggs. We should be cutting it close, but I think we'll make it."

"We'll run a decontamination sweep after they're gone. It doesn't work on the full-grown ones, but it should wipe out any nests they've left behind."

"Aye, ma'am."

Clare crossed her arms over her chest and looked around the bridge. She hated being cut out, hated having to wait for something else to happen. She was not going to be happy in the captain's chair. She reached up to hook her finger under her collar and began to pace.

Thetis held her cupped hands in front of her, curved so that the flame of her candle reflected on her fingers. Her eyes were closed, her lips moving silently as she spoke a prayer.

She didn't know what exactly the crew was planning, but there was a definite sense of activity and anxiety aboard. Something was happening, and it had something to do with the dark beast souls she had been sensing.

Thetis prayed for the crew's protection, with special focus on the safety of Clare and Anais.

Josiah Harp never planned to join Peaceful Sea. His father was a musician, and he'd taken his son to every rehearsal and performance trying to stoke a love of music in him. Harp hadn't been impressed with the act of making music, but the instruments themselves were beautiful, amazing things. He learned all about them, and how they made the beautiful melodies with just a burst of air and finger movement. In thousands of years, as everything else changed and evolved, music remained the same. His favorites were the woodwinds.

He could hear Harvestmen in the walls and ran faster.

Woodwinds. He thought about woodwinds as he ran, pumping his arms in time with his legs. He passed doors that had been locked on his orders, and he could hear the nightmare beasts keeping pace with him inside the walls. His face burned, and sweat dripped down his cheeks to pool on the collar of his uniform shirt. He had to make it to the hangar or everything would be for naught. He heard something smash into the corridor behind him, and he twisted to fire. The Harvestman was larger than he expected, and *green*.

He had dreams of a little shop where he could make instruments. Nothing fancy, and only on-world customers. He barely even thought of interstellar travel much, in those days.

Harp turned and strafed the corridor behind him with fire from his Fore-Arm. The pursuing pair of Harvestmen fell back, but one's head exploded with a satisfying crack.

One down.

When he was seventeen, he got into a disagreement. It involved gambling, and debts, and now that he was older and wiser he could admit he was in the wrong. He'd paid his debt with his right hand.

A doctor managed to reattach it, but he could never quiet get it to follow his mental commands. The precision work necessary for making instruments became impossible and, in a deep depression, he enlisted in the military.

Forty years later, and almost that long since he had last touched a woodwind, he burst into the wide open space of the hangar with slavering beasts in hot pursuit. He ran for a shuttle that had been left open in anticipation of his arrival, and he rushed inside. He shot another Harvestman in the side, severing its arm, as the doors finally closed with a solid thud. He was drenched with sweat, and his heart was hammering against his ribs. He felt lightheaded and weak, and his throat was too tight to draw air.

He managed to move to the front of the shuttle and looked outside. A Harvestman launched at the front window, claws scrambling over the smooth surface as it moved onto the top of the shuttle. Harp sank into the pilot's seat and tried to slow his breathing as he watched the aliens spread across the hangar in front of him. He counted six, the majority of them smaller than he'd ever seen.

Babies. Born hungry.

He could hear them skittering across the top of the shuttle, heard the impacts as they shoved their bodies against the side of the ship. He watched the entrance to the hangar and, when a full minute had gone by without any further arrivals, he turned on the control panel. He thumbed the emergency key, disabling the protocols so he could fire up the engines despite the hangar door being down.

He brought his radio up. "I hope they taught you to understand English, you assholes. Because you only have about twenty seconds to kiss your ugly asses goodbye."

The hangar doors slammed shut as the biohazard alert was activated. The screeching of the Harvestmen increased, and he saw them flee the shuttle and began scrambling for escape. Even Harvestmen didn't move fast enough, and their suddenly meager legs collapsed under their weight. Harp smiled as he watched the Harvestmen die, and he sagged against the back of his seat.

"That's right," he wheezed. "Try and take over *my* fucking ship..."

He closed his eyes as the chemicals breached the shuttle's hull. He lifted his right hand and pressed the Fore-Arm barrel into the soft skin above his throat. He didn't really want to know what it felt like to be dissolved.

EPILOGUE: FINALITY

I can only apologize to the families of the crewmembers who died on this foolhardy quest. I bear the full responsibility for what happened to them. It is my duty to protect my ship, my crew, from danger to the best of my ability. I cannot leave them in danger if it is within my power to save them. I can safely say it is fully within my power to do this. I have faith this plan will be successful, and I would not and could not ask anyone else to make the necessary sacrifice. To those who would consider reviving this abhorrent experiment in the future, I can only say that you should think of the innocent people who gave their lives in the past few years and rethink the weight of your soul. In closing, I hereby grant the rank of Captain to Rani Clare Cossin, and I leave my ship in her capable hands.

~ Captain Josiah Harp's final communication to his superiors

Clare ordered the ship's lockdown to continue while security forces checked level by level to ensure none of the enemy had survived. Hazardous Waste teams destroyed the only nest they knew about, and no other evidence of eggs was discovered. Kira volunteered to walk through various levels with her headset off and reported that she heard (and smelled) nothing out of the ordinary. Clare had Anais set a course for the nearest base, transmitted her report of everything that happened, and waited for the shit storm to begin.

When they arrived at Trivedi Base, the entire command staff was taken into "protective" custody and isolated so they could relay their portion of the story. All passengers were removed from the ship and the oxygen was replaced by a gas that would snuff out any remaining creatures. While the ship was cleaned out, Clare was officially promoted to Captain and given command of the *Paralus* as per the previous commander's wishes. She was granted a new first officer, an Indian woman transferred from the *Meridies* named Muriel Parekh.

The attempt by ACRA to reintroduce a weaponized version of Harvestmen into the universe was officially disavowed. The experiments were blamed on a radical division of scientists who were all imprisoned for their part in the mass deaths aboard the *Prospekt* and the *Juno*, as well as the casualties suffered by the *Paralus* crew.

During their sequestration, Clare and Anais continued exploring their physical relationship. Clare initially frowned on the idea of a captain sleeping with a member of her crew, but Anais wisely pointed out how often male captains got away with the same thing without controversy, and Clare relaxed. The girl was surprising in her abilities, sometimes requesting moves even Clare had never heard of, and she found herself emotionally at peace for the first time since Laikyn disappeared.

Clare's silence on the Harvestman matter was bought when the fallen crews were officially declared as having fallen in battle and were given full honors. A government funeral was announced, and Clare attended as a family member in civilian dress to honor her partner.

With the majority of the horror swept under the rug, the *Paralus* launched again five months after arriving on the base. Their first day out, Clare summoned the courage to visit Thetis in her quarters. The entire room had now been transformed, and it looked like a section of another ship had been grafted onto the hull.

"Your sanctuary is beautiful, Thetis."

She smiled. "Thank you, Captain. I've had a lot of time to prepare it."

"That's why I'm here." The Peaceful Sea and ACRA governments had wanted everyone on board the ship during the attacks to be sequestered on Trivedi until the matter was concluded. That meant Thetis was denied passage on other vessels that could have taken her to her people. "Obviously you've been extraordinarily inconvenienced by this whole mess. I wanted to apologize in person for everything, and ask if there was anything we could do to make amends."

Thetis considered the question, pausing to light a candle before she stood to face Clare. "There is no reason to apologize, Captain. Our people have been relocated to a new world to await the resurrection of our home. Do you know why I remained behind so long? Why I pushed my prayers and meditation to the point of risking my own life?"

"I don't know. Stubborn?"

"Hm. Yes. Quite a lot of that, actually. But I was praying for guidance. For a sign to show me where I was supposed to go. I thought your arrival, your urging me to come with you, was a sign that I was meant to join the others on our temporary planet. But now I see that the sign was... to come here. To this ship. So if you would be so kind as to contact my Regent and tell him I won't be coming... I would be obliged."

Clare said, "You want to stay?"

"With your blessing, of course. I would earn my passage~"

"It's not that." She wet her lips. "Is this about... us? And what happened?"

Thetis nodded. "Partially. I care very deeply for you, Clare. I know that you're currently mourning a tremendous loss, but perhaps in time you will be more comfortable with the thought of moving on." She held up her robes and crossed the room. Clare let Thetis touch her cheek, bracing only slightly when she leaned forward and kissed her. Clare forced herself to relax, closing her eyes before she parted her lips and touched her tongue to Thetis'. It was still odd, still not quite normal enough to completely relax, but it was... nice. Thetis broke the kiss and pressed her lips to the corners of Clare's mouth.

"I would like to be here whenever you are ready, Clare."

"Yeah. I think I would like that, too."

Thetis smiled and dipped her chin.

"You should know... ah." She cleared her throat. "Anais and I are in a relationship. So if you and I were to start anything, it would have to include her."

"I understand. Anais and I have already spoken on the matter."

Clare raised an eyebrow. "Have you. Well. I'll have to have a word with her about that." She touched Thetis' cheek. "It's easier.

Losing Laikyn. It's easier with you here. And Anais."

"We're not going anywhere, dear." She stepped back and squeezed Clare's hands. "Go now. You have a ship to guide."

She nodded once and left the quarters, waiting for the sound of the doors closing before she walked away. So she had been kicking herself about leading Thetis on while she was growing closer to Anais, and they were talking behind her back. She would have to have a discussion with Anais about that. She smiled as she stepped onto the lift and considered the ways they could make it up to her.

On the bridge, Commander Parekh rose from the captain's chair. Clare, still a touch wary about calling it her seat, nodded her thanks and sat down. They had a group of monks waiting on Elkepp for their traditional pilgrimage, and on the way they had to swing by to check on a solar array with a computer system that was sending back buggy information. She ran her hands over the armrests and settled into the curve of the seat.

"At your leisure, Captain."

Clare raised an eyebrow at Commander Parekh. "Watch that tone, new girl."

Parekh smirked and moved to her own station.

Clare looked around the bridge and then touched her earpiece. "Anais? Take us out of here, please."

"Aye-aye, babycakes."

Clare rolled her eyes. It was going to be an odd ship, but she doubted it would ever be boring. She smiled as their engines lit up and the *Paralus* set off on its next mission.